Marked

McKenna Rae

Prologue

May 26, 1880

I woke up that morning to my home being eerily quiet. Usually, the house was abuzz with servants working to keep the giant castle clean, or keep its occupants fed. At the very least I expected to hear my sister's singing, but there was nothing. I scooted to the edge of my bed before jumping down to the cold, wooden floor. Looking outside of my window I saw the sun high in the sky. It was a few hours past dawn which means the house should be a lot more active than it was.

My mind immediately went to the worst-case scenario. What if something bad had happened to everyone while I was sleeping? What if I would never see them again? Mommy and daddy, Cira, all the nice servants who had been around my whole life, what if they were all gone? I raced out of my room and down the hall, taking the steps on the grand staircase two at a time. I ran as fast as my little legs would allow me until I made it to the dining room where my parents sat eating their breakfast.

I sighed with relief when I saw them. Mommy with her beautiful chocolate brown wavy hair with its pretty, but odd white streak in the front piled on top of her head and held into place with a million tiny pins. Her fair skin, bright red lips, and long painted fingernails, flipped through the large stack of papers in front of her. She looked the picture of elegance as always with the finest dress paired with the shiniest of jewels.

Daddy, who chose to go for a more causal appearance for breakfast this morning with his lose fitting buttoned shirt and messy black hair that looked like he had recently run his hands through it multiple times. He studied his newspaper like he did every morning. Everything seemed normal but something did not feel right.

Slowly I approached my father. "Daddy," I called to him. He shuffled his newspaper to the side slightly so he could look at me with those bright blue, grey eyes. He raised one eyebrow waiting for me to continue. "Where is everyone? Why is it so quiet?" He pulled his newspaper back in front of his face once I had finished my question, like I had not even said anything at all.

I turned to my mother expecting her to respond to me but all she gave me was a cold, blank stare. "Mommy, where is Cira?" I asked looking around the dining room expecting her to appear.

It was strange enough that I did not hear her singing voice that I was so accustomed to waking up to but to not see her sharing breakfast with my parents was very strange.

My mother frowned. "We are in mourning" she said.

"Mourning?" I asked.

"Your sister is no longer with us." At her words my heart began beating rapidly, the color drained from my face, and I could feel this cold sickly feeling creep up my spine. Cira was gone? I would never see her again?

"You're lying!" I shouted. I refused to believe the lies they were telling me. She would never just leave me alone. With them. The same people who have kept me indoors since birth, never allowing me to enjoy the outside world with other children my age. Who has drilled the laws of our kind and my responsibilities into me for years. No, Cira would never just leave me, something was wrong.

"I want to see her!" I stomped my foot on the ground, letting them know I was not letting this go so easily.

"Enough!" My mother said getting to her feet and making her way around the table to me. She kneeled at my level and looked me in the eye. "She is gone, and you will never see her again. Cira has broken one of our most sacred rules and you will be wise not to follow in her footsteps lest the same fate be brought down upon you."

Her eyes softened as she placed her hand on my shoulder. "Niyla my sweet, do not make me mourn both of my daughters." I knew I was meant to obey her warnings because she was trying to protect me and at the time, as confused as I was, I thought that I would listen to her, we all thought this would be enough. How wrong we all turned out to be.

Chapter 1

June 6, 2019

I dreaded this day every year that it insisted on coming around. Sometimes I even tried to pretend the entire world would just forget I existed. My family, however, never failed to make a big deal about this horrible day. I stood in front of a full-length mirror, checking over my appearance. The floor-length, lacy, white dress did nothing to flatter the assets I wish were of more use to me. My lanky, olive skin toned arms hung loosely at my sides. They were on further display thanks to my lack of sleeves.

Why my parents insisted on putting me through this year after year I couldn't say, but this year would be different. This year I would get my chance to be free. No more dresses, no more grand parties, no more introductions to different high-ranking officials under my father's employ. I would get to live as I want for this one year and I was planning to take full advantage of it.

I smoothed down my dress once more and made sure my deep brown curls were secured nice and tight in the bun on top of my head before I deemed myself presentable enough to leave my room. I turned around to face my bedroom door just as I heard a slight knock followed by a very timid "Excuse me?"

I could hear the rapid heartbeat of the person on the other side of the door and smell the very strong body spray that exuded from their body. It was Harper, a long-time family acquaintance and pretty much my only friend. "Come in" I called. The door creeped open, and she slowly made her way inside. Her bright fire red hair brushed the collar of her white button up blouse. Those brown eyes I was always so jealous of remained cast down at the floor like always.

Harper was always so timid and shy. If you combined the way she acted with the way she looked you would never think that she was 250 years older than me, I guess that's one of the perks of being an immortal. "Your father has sent me to retrieve you, they are ready for you Niyla." She said in that same small voice I was so used to hearing. Thank the gods for my enhanced hearing abilities. I sighed and looked down at my appearance once more before reminding myself that after today I wouldn't have to deal with this anymore.

"Ok, I'm ready." She lifted her head slightly so she could look over my appearance before giving me a small smile. I took that as confirmation that I was good to go, and we both exited my bedroom. That same bedroom I called mind for more than 50 years and if I had my way would hopefully never call mine again.

From the top of the grand staircase, I could hear all the commotion. There were hundreds of different voices all speaking at the same time and not surprisingly from what I could pick up none of them had me as their topic of conversation. Slowly I took my first step then my next. It wasn't until I had made it halfway down the stairs that someone noticed my presence.

"I see the guest of honor has finally decided to grace us with her presence." Came the deep baritone voice I'd grown up listening to my entire life. My father, the honorable Ezra Gray, emerged from the crowd dressed in his immaculate, finely pressed tuxedo. His midnight black locks gelled back to give the illusion of the merciful gentlemen that he liked the world to perceive him as. All eyes turned toward me. You would think having this kind of attention for all these years would mean I'm accustomed to it, I am not. "My darling daughter, let me be the first to wish you a Happy Birthday." He held out his hand for me and I hesitated before making my way down the last few steps and crossing the distance to him.

When my hand landed in his, the entire room erupted in applause. I knew none of the people that filled the room, but then again, I never did. They were always only the people my parents deemed fit enough to invite into the inner circle, but with that being said, it never seemed to be the same people every time.

Every time my parents called a gathering, every person in attendance was a new person they struck some sort of alliance with. Rather they were from other high-ranking families or those my father chose to do business with. Who only knows what happened to the people they grew tired of and made vanished from their lives.

"Esteemed guests, I would like to introduce you all to the birthday girl, my lovely daughter, Niyla Gray. Today will be her last day in this house for an entire year. She plans to travel for the time being and return to us in time to fulfill her duties as a member of this family and this community." The crowd cheered again, and I even heard a few congratulations and good lucks.

"Now, if I may be so bold as to have this first dance?" He said it like it was meant to be a question, but we both knew the truth. I had no say in anything that was going to happen this evening. That was the deal, I grin and bear it, let my parents do whatever and say whatever they wanted for this last day, and they had no say in what I chose to do the year I was away from them. I wanted that freedom, I needed that freedom so for now

I would be their little puppet, playing the dutiful, obedient daughter.

I plastered on a smile and bowed to my father before he scooped me into his arms and began gliding me across the dance floor. From the corner of my eye, I could see the crowd staring at us in awe. They were really buying into all of this, so much so that it was almost laughable. "Your smile is slipping my daughter" My father whispered to me. I could feel myself clenching my teeth. My temper was starting to get the better of me, so I had to reign it in. Just focus on the end goal, freedom, even if it was only for a short while.

"My apologies Father, I must've forgotten my head for a second." The look on his face told me that I was not fooling him at all. He knew exactly where my train of thought was leading me.

"Do not let it happen again. You know our arrangement, if you do not hold up your end, your mother and I will not hold up ours." The coldness in his voice told me that he was 100% serious about his threat.

"Of course, it is only fair." I tried to resist the urge to clench my teeth even more. Any harder and I was sure I would chip a fang.

The amount of hatred and resentment I'd developed for my parents over the years was enough to almost scare even me. It started years ago, and it seemed to only grow every passing day that I spend with them. Some days I've even thought about ending them but knowing that there was no possible way I could do it alone. They were much too strong for me, and they had the fear of everyone in our community. I was completely alone in this battle to get out from under their control.

I straightened my back and tried to talk myself in to not embarrassing my father by cutting this dance short and leaving him in the middle of the dance floor with a furious expression on his face.

"Father if I might ask, what is it exactly you expect of me this evening. I've put on the dress you wished for me to wear, I've styled my hair as you requested, I've smiled and been otherwise polite. Now, I wonder what it is you hope to accomplish with this over-the-top birthday celebration that you know I absolutely hate." To say all of that while still trying to maintain that masking smile was a very tiresome task.

My father let out a sigh as if just the thought of answering my question was exhausting in itself. "My darling daughter," he said before spinning me out and bringing me back in to dip me. "It almost sounds as if you think I have hidden motives for this evening. Is it not enough for a father to want to spoil his only child with the birthday gathering he feels she deserves."

My smile slipped from my face, and I yanked my hands free of his. How could he say such a lie and to my face at that. I took a step toward him and gathered on the balls of my feet so I could whisper into his ear. "I am not your only child." I spat out. He and my mother had been trying to play this game with me for over a hundred years. They tried constantly to erase the truth from my mind. My older sister Cira existed no matter how hard they tried to make it seem like she did not.

They removed pictures, they destroyed every personal item she had left in our home as well as executing anyone who so much as uttered her name on the spot. No, they would not erase her from my mind, I don't care what they tried to do. "The sooner you get it through your head that she existed the sooner I'll stop thinking of you as a sociopath who only cares about controlling those around them."

I could feel the tears welling up in my eyes, but I refused to let anyone see me cry. The weak girl everyone tried to keep in her place had long since disappeared years ago and would never again return. I gave my father a quick peck on the cheek for appearances, took a step back, and gave a quick curtsy before turning and walking away from him.

I wasn't sure what the look on his face was, but I know as angry as I'm sure he was, he wouldn't show it in front of all the guests he'd invited here.

Fresh air was what I needed. This stupid party had only just begun and already I was feeling suffocated. I know my parents were up to something by planning this right before I leave for my year off however, I don't know why I expected to get a straight answer out of them. I made my way out to the back patio. The fact that there were tables and chairs, hundreds of bright string lights and even an entire buffet set up, told me that at some point the party was scheduled to move outdoors.

I paced back and forth across the patio trying to get my thoughts together. My anger and frustration were getting the better of me and I didn't want to risk my parents reneging on their end of the deal and preventing me from leaving. Taking a few deep breaths, I closed my eyes and tried to imagine what the world would be like outside of this wretched castle. Off this isolated island.

"The birthday girl shouldn't be out here alone at her own party." A raspy voice said from behind me, followed by a slight knock against the wood paneling of the door frame. My back stiffened; I didn't recognize the voice, but I really wasn't in the mood to play nice with any of my father's suck ups. I especially wasn't in the mood if my father had sent him out here to keep an eye on me and make sure I didn't do anything foolish to spoil his evening.

Slowly I turned to face the man. Blonde, curly hair, dark eyes, incredibly fair skin, and a lot of facial hair. If I didn't know any better, I could swear he was a werewolf and not a vampire. If the rumors I use to hear were true and they did in fact exist.

"Who are you?" I asked. He gave me a small smile and took a step towards me.

"My apologies, my name is Laurel. I am to be your escort this evening." I couldn't help the growl that escaped me.

"I don't know what story my father has spun for you, but I do not need an escort. Now, please go back and convey that message to him." He could also convey a couple other choice words, but I'd rather not poke the bear.

His smile grew wider. "You misinterpret me my sweet," There was a sick feeling that entered my stomach with the way he seemed so familiar when speaking with me. Who was he and why did he feel like he had the privilege of speaking to me in such a manner. "I am one of your potential destined. To be decided once you've returned."

In that moment it seemed as if all the air had been sucked from my lungs. I hadn't heard him correctly, I couldn't have. I was sure this had to be a joke but the longer I stared at his un-wavering smile, I knew that he spoke the truth. My father had once again lied to me. This party wasn't just a simple birthday party for me, it wasn't even his last chance to parade me around in front of all his subordinates before I took off for the year, no, this was another party full of suitors for me, but from the looks of it this time I wouldn't get a say in if I wanted one or not. This party is one big, arranged marriage meeting. This was his plan all along, this is what he meant when he said fulfill my duty as a member of this community. I was just another political tool for him.

"Niyla, are you feeling, ok? You look a little queasy." Laurel said as he took another step towards me.

I swallowed deeply trying to process everything. "Come near me and I will rip out your intestines and feed them to you." My jaw ached from the force of me trying not to extend my fangs and drain the life from his veins. I wanted to kill this man and every other who was here for the same reason as he, but what I wanted the most was to get away from here and I wanted to do it now. I refuse to wait until the party concluded, I was leaving the moment I could slip away.

Chapter 2

"Niyla you cannot be serious about this ludicrous plan." Harper rushed out in an urgent tone. She had followed me from the ballroom all the way back to my bedroom.

"I can assure you; I am very serious." The bags I luckily already had packed for tonight were waiting for me by my bed. All that was left now was to get out of this ridiculous dress and out of this soul sucking house.

It had become very clear that this year off was just that, a YEAR off. Once I returned, I would never be free of my parent's control. If I didn't escape now, I would never be allowed to.

"What is your plan, Niyla? Your parents will notice you're gone, and they will find you. Your best solution is to finish the evening then leave like you planned." While Harper continued to be futile in her efforts to talk me out of this very risky plan, I continued rummaging through my closet trying to find the most inconspicuous pieces of clothing I owned.

"I don't have a plan; all I know is that if I stay here, they'll never let me leave." Finding a black, long-sleeved shirt and a pair of dark jeans, I quickly got changed.

"Don't be ridiculous, of course they are going to let you leave. They told you if you did what they said you would be free to leave tonight. If you leave now, that all goes away." I didn't have time to stand here and argue with her. This is the influence that my parents have on the people around them. They give you the illusion of good people who hold up to their word, but the reality is they are nothing but lying monsters who I absolutely believe had something to do with the disappearance of my sister.

I will not allow them to keep up with this lie any longer and I will not let them keep me locked up here for the rest of my existence.

"Harper, you are not going to talk to me out of this. My decision is final so either help me or leave." I looked her straight in the eye and dared her to say another word in defense of my horrid parents.

She dropped her eyes and sighed. "I won't stop you, but I can't help you either. I have been an ally to this family for almost 2 centuries, I cannot simply betray your parents. I will not aid you, but your parents will find out nothing from me." I guess that is to be expected. My parents took her in when she needed it the most. Years ago, at a time before I was born, when our people were hunted and slaughtered by the hundreds, my parents gave her refuge so it only makes sense that she would choose them over me. It doesn't make it hurt any less though.

I finished changing, yanked out all the pins in my hair and tied it into a loose ponytail. "So, what is your plan?" She asked. I eyed her suspiciously. She had already admitted to siding with my parents, would it really be wise to tell her my entire escape plan?

She noticed my look and gave me an eye slant that told me she was annoyed at where my mind was going. "Niyla, don't be daft. I said I would not aid you, but I also said your parents will never know anything from me." When I still didn't speak of my plan, she took a step toward me and sat on the edge of my bed. "I've known you since you were born, you know you can trust me. I just want to make sure you're safe."

I was still very cautious about telling her what I planned to do, but if I don't go into too many details, it should be ok. "I need to get to the docks." Even as I said it, I was racking my brain trying to figure out how to get there undetected. It would take hours to walk there and by that time, I would've been found out and it would take nothing for them to catch up to me. I couldn't use my speed because it would exert too much of my energy and I wasn't sure when I would be able to feed again, so what other options did I have.

"Some of the guests used cars to travel from the other side of the island, take one of their cars." She said after a moment of silence. "I can get you the keys. You take their car because it can't be tracked like your parent's can. Take it to the pier and hop one of the exporting ships. Don't tell me which one."

"Why are you helping me? I thought you said you wouldn't do anything to betray my parents." She smiled at me and reached for my hand. I gave it to her, and she squeezed tight.

"I did say I would not betray your parents, but I cannot betray you either. If you truly believe this is the only way I will do whatever I have to, to ensure your safety." She pressed her lips to the back on my hand before getting to her feet.

"Now, you must be quick. It won't be long before they realize you're no longer downstairs you must hurry." I rushed over and grabbed my backpack. I had more luggage, but it was clear I needed to travel as light as possible. Just the essentials. "Climb out your window and wait by the bushes. I will get the keys and meet you there." As soon as she said that she was gone in a flash.

I've never had a need to open my bedroom window in all the years I had lived in this house, but it didn't take me long to figure out how to jimmy the lock open and get the window up. The drop from my window to the patch of grass down below wasn't that great of a distance, but still with nothing to cushion my fall from a fourth story window I was going to get hurt. The injury wouldn't last long with my healing abilities, but it would be a factor in slowing me down for sure.

I tossed my bag down first but looking at the tiny black dot surrounded by all the green, it was obvious it wasn't going to provide enough of a cushion. Grabbing a couple of pillows off my bed, I tossed those down too. Sadly, those weren't going to work either. I couldn't keep wasting time like this. Harper could be waiting for me right now and if she was caught, not only would she be severely punished for trying to help me escape, but any chance I had at freedom would all be gone.

Deciding I had no other choice, I climbed up on my windowsill and let my legs dangle over the edge. The pain wouldn't last long. I told myself this repeatedly before taking a deep breath and jumping. The cold, hard ground came a lot quicker than I was expecting it too and so did the pain that started at my ankle and spread all the way up to my knee. I groaned and rolled onto my side, clutching my leg.

Suck it up Gray, you must keep moving. Harper is risking her life for you; you can't keep her waiting. Mustering up all the strength my sheltered little self could, I made it to my feet, grabbed my bag and slowly made my way around to the other side of the house. I moved as quietly as I could, sticking close to the brick wall where there was the most cover from the lights.

Finally, when it seemed like I had been creeping around for hours, I made it to the bushes. Harper stood there, scanning the area intensely. I whispered her name and luckily, she heard me because her eyes immediately met mine. There was relief on her face as she quickly made her way over to me and shoved the keys in my hands.

"You're running out of time. You must move quickly. Already I have heard whispers of people questioning your disappearance. It won't be long before your father comes to look for you." Her head snapped in the direction of the back patio where already guests had begun making their way to the buffet.

"What about you?" I asked. "I don't think it's safe for you to stay behind."

She gave me a sad smile, one that told me there was nothing I could do to convince her that coming with me was a lot safer than staying behind and suffering the wrath of my mother and father. "You know this journey is one you must take on your own. I must stay behind and do my best to make sure that you are not found for as long as possible." She raised her hand to my face and brushed my cheek. "This may be the last we see of each other. You will not come back to this place, ever, do you understand?"

I hesitated but knew that even coming this far meant that there was no turning back, so I nodded and made the vow to never see her or this house again. "Now go, quickly!" I gave her one final hug before making my way as quickly as I could on my bum leg to the front where all the guests had left their cars.

Hitting the button on the key ring, an all-black Mercedes lit up and I limped towards it. Luckily the guards were around back with the rest of guests, otherwise I had no idea how I was getting pass them.

I climbed into the driver's seat and started up the car. It hummed quietly and I couldn't help but enjoy the adrenaline I was feeling that this was happening. With one final look at the house that had kept me caged for so long, I put the car in reverse and backed out of the driveway. I mentally said one final goodbye to Harper as I pulled off, watching the house disappear in the rear-view mirror.

The docks where I would make my long-awaited escape, seemed to be hours away but I know they weren't more than half an hour away from the place I called home. The anticipation of getting there made the drive seem to take forever and the paranoia that I was being followed did not help to calm my nerves.

When I saw the exhaust from the ships over the horizon, it felt as if a weight had been lifted off my shoulders. I was almost there; I was almost free. So far everything had gone according to plan. That's what I thought anyway until my bag made a beeping noise. I reached for the side pocket and pulled out my cellphone. Clicking on the screen, I read the message in bold letters, it was Harper.

They know! They're coming for you!

My heart jumped out of my chest. How did they find out so quickly? Do they know where I am? How long did I have before they found me? So many questions raced through my head. I can't go back I told myself as I stepped on the gas and raced down the road. The ships grew bigger the closer I got until eventually they loomed over me.

I made it, all I needed to do now was sneak on board and hope I wasn't found before the ship set sail. That shouldn't be too hard, I made it this far. I parked the car off into the shadows, just a few feet before reaching the pier. I could hear the different ship's crew working diligently to get the vessels prepared to reset sail.

Which one do I take? I didn't exactly have a printout of where each ship was heading. No choice, I had to pick one. Anyone. Before getting out of the car I rotated my ankle a little trying to test my injury. Already it was feeling a lot better.

Feeling a little more confident, I grabbed my bag, got out of the car, and headed straight for the biggest ship in the entire pier. Hopefully the biggest ship travels the furthest because I needed to put as much distance between me and my family as I possibly could.

No one guarded the boats and as I walked up the ramp that put me right on deck, no one questioned my appearance. I knew eventually someone would notice I was out of place, and I would be turned in, so I had to hide. I looked around the big, rusty, metal boat, taking in my surroundings. There were crates and giant metal storage containers everywhere. At the front of the ship, a huge metal tower stood but even from this distance, I could see someone was up there.

At the other end of the ship a wall so high I couldn't see if there was anything on the other side. Hundreds of tiny windows scattered throughout and at the top, a long row of big, bright lights. That wouldn't be the ideal place to hide either. My only other choice was to hide between the large metal storage containers and hope nobody found me. So that's exactly what I did.

I found a tiny space between two containers and slipped between them. It wasn't the most comfortable spot, but I hoped it would at least be sufficient during the journey across the sea. Not long after getting settled into my hiding space, I heard the loud blare of the horn, and the boat began to move.

I couldn't see land from where I was, but I knew that the land I called my home for so many years was getting smaller and smaller the further away the shipped moved.

Finally, I was getting my freedom, finally I could say goodbye to my home.

Chapter 3

How long had it been since I came up with the bright idea of taking a ship across the ocean. Someone who's never even seen a boat in person let alone been out on the water. I felt horrible, nauseous, lightheaded, but most of all I was hungry.

The sun had come up and gone down twice since I left home, and in that time, I had eaten every single snack bar I had packed but still my stomach ached for more.

I know what I needed even though after all my years living, I had never once starved for it or been denied it. Blood. I needed blood and I needed it now. I couldn't think straight, all my plans for escape were pushed to the back of my mind to make room for all the cravings my body was having.

The ship docked after two days at a pier in the middle of the night. There were no people on the dock only the ship workers loading and unloading crates from the ship. I scootched forward inch by inch from my hiding place between the two metal crates, trying to get a better view of where I was and who was around. My body ached from the cramped position I had been in for hours and without the blood my system needed, the injury to my leg I got when I jumped out of my bedroom window hadn't healed properly. Getting to my feet made for a pretty difficult task. Not only was my leg still torn up, but I also had what I heard some of the workers refer to as sea legs. I couldn't seem to keep myself steady.

Somehow, I managed to get to my feet and make it to the edge of the ship where the workers were unloading some of the crates. I noticed some of them staring at me in confusion. One of the workers even approached me.

"Hey! You can't be here." He shouted at me. When I looked at him, his face was blurry. I leaned against the metal edging of the boat, trying to will my vision to become clear again.

"Did you hear what I said?" He came closer and waved his finger in my face. "How did you get onboard?" He asked. When I didn't answer, he grew more agitated and instead of attempting to talk to me any longer, he grabbed me by my arm and pulled me to the ramp that led from the boat to the dock.

"Off now!" He shouted in my face. I guess the pace I was moving at wasn't sufficient for him, because after I had only taken a few steps down the ramp, he pushed me the rest of the way.

My body lurched forward, and I tumbled toward the dock. I closed my eyes and braced for the inevitable impact of my body hitting the wooden boards, but instead I landed on something softer. Strong arms wrapped around my body and pulled me close. My skull rattled and ached but still I tried to force my eyes open so I could look at the person who saved me from what I am sure would've been a very painful experience.

I could barely make out their features when my already blurry vision began to darken. I tried fighting off the sleepy feeling I suddenly had, but my body felt so heavy and all I wanted to do was close my eyes and hope that when I woke up, I would feel a million times better than I did at this very moment.

How long I slept, I have no idea, but I woke in an unfamiliar place on an unfamiliar bed, the first thoughts that came to mind was that I had managed to be found and they had taken me back. Considering I didn't recognize any of my surroundings, I felt the smallest amount of relief that wasn't the case.

Sitting up more, I took in my surroundings which was kind of hard to do since my head was still swimming. White walls surrounded me, a small black leather sofa sat in one corner of the room near a small metal end table. The bed I laid on took up the rest of the space. Four mahogany bed posts and black cotton sheets was all I could see. The bed was huge. Overall, the room was very sparsely decorated. Just a few black out curtains to cover the small round windows that looked out into the night.

"Finally, you're awake," a deep, masculine voice spoke, shaking me to my core. I flinched and looked around for the voice, but I couldn't see who it was. "I was worried I would have to explain to the police that a stow-away died on my ship." Finally, a blurry figure came into view. I hadn't noticed the door in the far corner, opposite the small couch. He emerged from the doorway of what I assume was a small bathroom. The moonlight shone through a crack in the curtain over the small window just as he took a step toward me, giving him a breathtaking glow.

Blonde hair, long and unkept, dark, narrow eyes, and muscles, lots of muscles. He wore a snug fitting, short sleeve, black t-shirt giving my still disoriented sight quite the view. His gorgeous appearance was so unexpected, it took a second for alarm bells to begin going off in my head. I tried moving as far away from him as I could but considering I was currently tangled in the bedsheets, that proved to be very difficult.

"Who are you?" I asked continuing to inch away the closer he got.

I heard a slight laugh as he set a small hand towel on the edge of the bed before sitting down on the footboard. "You don't remember anything do you?"

I still eyed him suspiciously but shook my head no. "One of my crewmen found you stumbling around my ship. He proved to be less then gentlemanly toward you with the way he tried to entice you to exit my vessel." He gave a slight shrug. "Lucky for you, I don't tolerate any abuse towards women and that particular crewman found himself hitting the dock before you did." I vaguely remember someone yelling at me and then being pushed, but after that, everything was a blank.

"How did I get here?" I asked. My voice cracked and it wasn't until now that I realized how dry my throat was.

"On my ship or in my bed?" He asked. His tone came off playful, but as much as he tried to hide it, I could tell he was a little annoyed.

He got to his feet and made his way around to the side of the bed, sitting entirely too close to me. I slid as far as I could to the other side of the bed trying to put more distance between us, but it didn't seem like it made much of a difference. As big as the bed was, this huge beast of a man seemed to take up the entire space.

"Obviously you hopped my ship at our last port because," he gave me a once over. "You definitely don't look like you're from around here." I looked down at what I was wearing. Still the same t-shirt and jeans. What was so bad about what I was wearing? Was I in some weird land where this wasn't considered normal, because last time I checked, he was basically wearing the same thing.

"I don't know what you're talking about." I raised my chin and looked him in the eyes, trying my hardest to make my voice sound even so he wouldn't sense the lies as they rolled off my tongue. "I've lived here my whole life and there's nothing wrong with my clothes." I folded my arms across my chest which I realized a little too late only succeeded in putting my breasts on full display for this strange man to ogle at. Yet another downside to being well endowed, they made situations like this very awkward. To his credit though, he did his best not to stare, not immediately anyway.

"Lived here all your life huh?" He eyed me suspiciously making my stomach do a little flip. I nodded immediately. Which in hindsight is probably what gave me away, I was too eager for him to believe me. "So, the backpack full of clothes is what?" He used his thumb to gesture toward my backpack that sat on the sofa behind him. "You're laundry?"

I swallowed the lump forming in my throat. He knows, he knows I ran away and he's going to turn me in. My mind was working a mile a minute as I tried to think of a solution to get out of this, but I was drawing a blank. My leg still throbbed in pain, and I still hadn't fed which means I was as weak as a normal human woman, if not weaker. There was no way I would be able to overpower this man and escape.

He stared at me, patiently waiting for an explanation meanwhile I was starting to realize, the longer we sat in silence the louder his heartbeat sounded to me. That strong heartbeat that pumped delicious blood throughout his entire body.

My mouth began to salivate but no matter how many times I swallowed; I couldn't seem to moisten my dry throat. The more we sat this close together in this confined space, the harder it was becoming to keep myself in check. Already I could feel my fangs lengthening so I tried my hardest to keep my mouth shut so he wouldn't see them.

"Are you okay?" He asked. He snapped his fingers in front of my face and it wasn't until that moment that I realized I had been staring at the pulsating vein in his neck. Every time it throbbed my stomach clenched. I wanted so bad to feed from it and at the current moment I couldn't think of any reason why I couldn't.

"I'm..." I could feel myself leaning forward. It didn't do much as far as closing the distance I had previously put between us, but each inch closer made the smell of his blood stronger. "I'm... I'm hungry."

Realization flashed across his face, and he nodded his head slightly. "Figures" he said running his hands through his golden locks. "If I'd acted like a stowaway on some strange ship for two days, I would be hungry too." He made a move to get off the bed and at a speed that couldn't be seen by the human eye, I reached out and grabbed his arm.

His head snapped back to look at where my hand connected with his arm. "What are you doing?" he asked, tugging his arm. I loosened my grip a little, giving him the impression that if he wanted to, he could get away. I didn't want to scare him, I also didn't want to bite him, but it was looking like I wouldn't get much of a choice in either matter.

"You haven't told me your name." I said I tried to feign innocence long enough for me to work up the courage to do what needed to be done. "If you saved me the way you claim you did, I should at least know your name, right?"

That suspicious look was back on his face but after a few seconds of hesitation, he decided to take his place back on the edge of the bed. "You can call me Kai." He finally spoke. "Now since we're sharing, are you going to tell me why you're on my ship." He pulled his arm from me and folded them both across his chest.

I scooted another couple of inches closer to him. Just need to keep him talking. "I'm hiding." It took every ounce of strength to break eye contact with his neck and look him in the eyes. Those beautiful eyes. Have I ever seen eyes so blue, the sea itself was probably green with envy.

He ran a hand through his blonde locks. "Look, we don't need any trouble," I scooted closer. "So, whatever you're hiding from" Closer. "You can't do it here." I closed those last few inches between us. My thigh brushed his hip.

I pulled his arm causing him to lean into me slightly. He smelled so good. I told myself just a little would be enough. Just enough so I could heal and that was it. I would leave this boat and never bother him again.

My pulse quickened the closer he got. I could hear his voice, but I couldn't hear what he was saying as my head fell into the crook of his neck and I inhaled his scent. My stomach seized and my heart sped up. I could feel the sweat begin to form on my brow, had it been this hot in here the whole time? I couldn't resist anymore. I had to have it. Now.

"I'm sorry" I whispered in his ear before I opened wide feeling my fangs extend and bit into his neck.

Chapter 4

Dropping the empty crates on the dock with a loud thump, I stood up and took off my work gloves before running my fingers through my blonde locks. It's been a while since I've cut it, but I usually didn't make it a habit until me and my crew got a break. Even for us, this had been an especially long voyage. Eight months, but finally we were on our last leg of it. Three more ports stood in between us and home.

"Captain!" One of my men shouted from onboard. "That was the last of it, we're ready to set sail when you are." I looked around at all the empty crates that sat at the edge of the dock, just to make sure we didn't miss one. Once I was satisfied, I stuffed my gloves into my back pants pocket before heading up the ramp.

"Did you hear what I said?" I looked up at the sound of a voice and saw one of my newest recruits, Julian. He was in his early 30s and had a bad temper. His bad temper mixed with his incredibly large build really made me question why I hired him in the first place. Call me a sucker for giving someone a chance.

His large frame prevented me from seeing who he was talking to, so I quickened my pace. I really didn't want to have to pull him off yet another member of the crew. The closer I got the more I noticed the crew begin to surround him and gawk at whoever he was talking to. He was causing an unnecessary spectacle, again.

The crew parted slightly and finally I could get a look at who the current victim of Julian's wrath was. Immediately, I stopped in my tracks. A woman.

She stumbled around trying to slowly make her way to the ramp. I watched as Julian walked up behind her physically getting more and more frustrated by how slowly she was moving. Alarm bells began going off in my head, making me quicken my pace.

"Off now!" I heard him shout as he used way too much force for a girl that size to shove her down the ramp. Her body jerk forward, she lost her footing and began to fall forward. I stood in the path of her fall and braced myself for the impact of her body against mine. She landed right against my chest, her body immediately going slack against me. The girl lifted her head slightly to look at me, her eyes an odd shade of gray. She leaned more against me before her eyes shut and her body went limp.

The rage that boiled inside of me was immediate and I looked up to glare at Julian. He stared back at me in shock.

"Miles!" I called for my right hand, and he appeared next to Julian immediately. I gestured toward the girl, and he got the hint, making his way down the ramp and reaching for the girl so I could have my hands free.

I never took my eyes off Julian as Miles lifted her weight from my chest. I hope he was scared. I don't have as big of a build as he does, I'm more on the slim side, but what I don't have in stature, I made up for in raw muscle. I never backed down from a fight and I sure as hell never tolerated any man putting his hands on a woman.

"C- Captain" He stammered out as I approached him. My crew parted to make way for me. They knew it was pointless to step in front of me because all it would do is make them end up with the same fate as him. "She was hiding onboard." He rubbed his hands against his pants and took a step back trying to put more distance between us, but all that would do is delay the inevitable. "You told us that there was no tolerance for anyone trying to catch a free ride." I continued to stalk towards him as his ramblings continued, none of which I was really listening to, there was no point. I saw what he did with my own eyes.

"So, your solution is to push a sick girl from the top of a seven-foot-tall ramp." He shook his head vigorously but before he could open his mouth to say anything else, I took a step forward and swung. My fist instantly connected with his jaw, and I heard the satisfying crunch of his jaw disconnecting from the rest of his skull.

The instant shriek came as I expected it to. Julian clutched his jaw and fell to the floor, rolling back and forth in agony.

"I want him off my ship." I said as I stared down at him, satisfied with the pain I had inflicted on him. My crew immediately jumped into action, grabbing him up and dragging him off the ship.

"What should we do with her?" Miles asked. He had lifted her into his arms and followed me onto the ship.

I looked her over. She looked like she couldn't be more then seventeen. Dark hair, Olive skin, not someone who looked like they were used to boat life.

"She got an ID?" Miles stretched out his arms for me to take her from him before going through the backpack she had been clutching when she fell. He dug around in it for a second before zipping it back.

"No ID, just a bunch of clothes. She might be a runaway." He said with a shrug.

"A runaway huh?" I looked her over once more, trying my hardest to imagine what she could possibly be running away from.

"So, what do we do now?" Miles asked.

"We don't know which port she came from, so we don't have any choice but to wait until she wakes. Until then, we set sail. We can't let this put us behind schedule." Miles gave me a nod before heading off to get the ship ready, leaving me alone with the mystery girl. She wouldn't be a mystery for long, I would make sure of it.

The moment his sweet blood touched my tongue, it was like pure euphoria. All my taste buds were buzzing, I could see stars behind my eyelids and every muscle in my body tightened. It was like a drug, and I couldn't get enough of it. I tried to pull him closer, to get more of this feeling, but just as quickly as it was there, it was gone. He pulled away ripping his neck from my lips.

I sat there stunned, staring at him. Not only was I shocked by his ability to wiggle out of my hold, but I was also having trouble coming to terms with my own reaction to not only him but his blood. I only needed a taste, that would've been enough to at least help with the healing process, but after that first drop touched my tongue I couldn't seem to stop. It was like drinking a gallon of water after being in the hot desert for 100 days without it. Like being blind and seeing the world for the first time. Like an addict that finally got their fix.

My body felt like it was vibrating. Everything felt hot, including that special place between my legs. My chest rose and fell as I tried to catch my breath and I couldn't contain the urge to stick my tongue out and lick any remaining blood from my lips.

"What did you do to me?" Came Kai's hoarse question after a few moments of silence. I jumped a little at hearing his voice. For a very few moments I had forgotten all about him, all I could think about was his blood. Even now, while I was slowly coming back to my senses, I could still hear the blood rushing through his veins and pumping his heart even faster. "You bit me." It was more of a statement than a question. I watched as he pulled the hand he kept clutched against the side of his neck away revealing a few drops of blood. My nostrils flared and I could feel myself moving towards him again. This time I didn't want his blood, I wanted something else.

Using my speed, I grabbed him by his shoulders and laid him flat on his back with me straddling his hips. His blood was still wreaking havoc on my senses, but now hunger wasn't my top priority. Not that kind of hunger at least. I stared down into his wide, unblinking eyes, but the fog in my head refused to lift. My body was completely running on autopilot as I pressed down against him, rubbing that sensitive place between my legs against him.

It felt like a jolt of electricity shot through my body and I realized I wasn't the only one whose body was reacting this way.

The hard outline of Kai's erection pressed against the tingling flesh between my legs causing more moisture to pool there. I pressed down again, but this time Kai meant me halfway, lifting his hips to meet mine.

He let out a groan and I was finding it increasingly hard to keep my eyes focused on him. He thrust his hips up again and my eyes closed, my head fell back. All my body wanted to do was feel and I was only too happy to oblige as we both continued to rub against each other.

I had never felt like this before, it felt like my heart was racing a mile a minute and I couldn't seem to catch my breath. My hips moved by themselves, and more and more moisture pooled between my legs.

This feeling was new to me, any interactions with the opposite sex was very limited for me. When I say limited, I mean just my father and any male suitor he deemed worthy, accompanied by his supervision obviously. These feelings I was having now, the fluttering in my stomach, the sweaty palms, the shortness of breath, the throb between my legs. They were exciting and scary, but most of all they felt amazing.

Looking down at Kai, I stared in awe at the way he looked as I grinded my body on top of him. His eyes closed, his mouth hanging open in a silent groan and his chest raising and falling rapidly. Was he enjoying this as much as I was? I pressed my center down harder against him, enjoying the jolt it sent up my spine, taking my breath away in the same instant. My mind was a blank slate except for one thing, I wanted his blood again.

That rich, sweet blood that I'd only gotten a small taste of before it was snatched away from me, I wanted more. I needed more. Between my legs a tingling sensation began, one I had never felt before. Moving harder and faster against Kai, I tried to make the tingling stop, but my actions only seemed to make it worse. A pressure began to build in my lower belly and the tingling intensified, like an itch I couldn't scratch.

My body, acting on its own leaned forward. I was once again lined up with the pulse on the side of his neck. I pressed my lips to the spot my fangs had previously touched and felt the tempting pulse against my lips. I felt his body jerk and he placed his hands on my hips, pulling me closer and tilting his head to the side exposing more of his neck to me, almost like he was asking me to bite him. I didn't need any further encouragement. I opened wide, letting my fangs extend and drove them into his neck.

One tug on the vein in Kai's neck as I took a big gulp of his blood, and he let out a groan followed by a shudder that racked through his entire body. Like a spring in my body that was coiled too tight, something snapped, and all the air rushed out of my lungs. My body mimicked his with shudder after shudder racing through my body.

My fangs retracted and like a pile of flesh, I laid on top of him completely unable to move and forced to bask in the euphoria I was suddenly feeling. Kai's grip on my hips had loosened but just like me, he couldn't seem to get his body to move. That is until a loud banging sound jolted us both.

"Captain are you alright? The crew is asking if you will be joining us for dinner?" At the sound of the voice, Kai jumped up effectively knocking me to the floor in the process.

He fussed with his clothing and even in the poor lighting provided by just the moon, my superior vision allowed me to see the very noticeable wet spot at the front of his pants. He let out a frustrated grunt before looking back at me. The angry scowl he gave me made my heart skip a beat and immediately pushed away the fog clouding my brain.

I was angry, frustrated and confused all at the same time. What the hell was this girl? In the short time since she had woken up, she'd gone from being cautious of me, to biting me, to dry humping me and then back to biting me.

"What kind of freak of nature are you?" I tried to keep my voice low in case any of my crew men were nearby.

She flinched before wiping her mouth with the back of her hand. Probably checking if any of my blood was left there. She opened her mouth to speak but I cut her off before she could.

"I don't know what you are but at the next port, I want you off this ship." I turned and stormed out before she had a chance to say anything, slamming the door behind me. I weaved through the corridor trying to make my way to the communal bathroom. There was no way I could show up to dinner in this state. My pants stuck to my thigh, causing me to shiver in disgust. My pants were mocking me and reminding me that someone my age shouldn't have let a girl who looked no more than seventeen stir me up this way.

I put one foot in front of the other trying to move quickly so I could make it to the bathroom before anyone saw me, something suddenly occurred to me. Each step I took further away from my room and that girl, a knowing feeling began to develop in the pit of my stomach. I couldn't describe it, almost like the sinking feeling you get when you're standing at the edge of a cliff.

I tried shaking it off, but the feeling stayed. What the hell did that girl do to me? Why did I get this feeling that if I didn't go back right now something bad was going to happen? I had this almost overwhelming urge to be around her and never leave her side. Instinctively my hand went up to the side of my neck, right where she had bitten me. I rubbed the spot, checking to see if there were any teeth marks left behind or seeing if there was still blood. I pulled my hand back and saw no blood. I let out a sigh of relief before opening the door to the bathroom and walking in.

I needed a shower bad, this sticky feeling on my thighs was starting to dry up which made it even more uncomfortable and would probably make it damn near impossible to take my pants off. Stepping over to the shower I reach for the handle and turned it letting the water steam up the small shower space while I stripped off my shirt and struggled to peel away my jeans.

That sinking feeling in my stomach only grew worse, I doubled over slightly and clutched at it. What was wrong with me? I had an almost overpowering urge to run but run away from what I didn't know. I took a deep breath before climbing into the shower and let the hot water run over my body. I tried to breathe through the discomfort I was feeling. I needed this feeling to dull enough so I could get my thoughts together.

The events of the last couple of hours played through my mind. This was supposed to be a routine trip, dock at the port, load up the cargo and then ship out. The receiving port was supposed to be in North America which meant my crew and I would get a couple days on land to visit family and relax before having to ship out again. When Julian found her, not only was I confused on how she even managed to not only sneak past the rest of the us but also how the hell she managed to stay hidden for that entire journey port to port. Besides confusion, I also felt immediate rage when I saw how he was handling her. If I hadn't caught her when I did, her brain would've been splattered all over the dock. My response of breaking his jaw and then throwing him off the ship might've been a little excessive even for me, but I couldn't stand to see a man hurt a defenseless woman.

We've all caught at least one stowaway on the ship before and have had to throw them off, but this was different. I didn't like seeing his hands on her. When I saw the way he shoved her, I could've torn his head off his shoulders.

I've never been the particularly chivalrous type, nor have I ever been the type to step foot in someone else's business, but I couldn't help but wonder what would make a girl like that hop a random ship headed God knows were by herself. It hadn't escaped my attention that she was quick to change the subject when I tried to get more information about who was chasing her. She did manage to distract me but that doesn't mean I forgot about it.

There was still a day and a half of travel before we hit our next port and if she was going to be aboard until then, I needed to know what kind of danger we might face once we got to the port. Before that though, I needed to know what kind of danger my crew faced onboard.

She bit me, she drank my blood. Any normal person would try to come up with some type of explanation for why she did what she did or what she is, but not me. Like a lot of other sailors, there were rumors going around about the island I suspected she came from. They were supposed to be just the drunken ramblings of sailors when they've had one too many. The tales were right up there with seeing Moby dick and buried treasure.

Apparently, there was supposed to be this ancient group of people that have lived on that island for centuries. Nobody knows where they came from or how long exactly, they had been there. One day, they just were. Those people had a name, vampire.

It's said that they don't take kindly to outsiders, and anyone that sets foot on their island never leaves. The only time anyone ever goes near that place is if there's a shipment and even then, there's never anyone there waiting at the docks. We're always just expected to unload the shipment and collect payment in the form of a wad of cash in a lock box right in the middle of the dock. It's all very sketchy. That girl is probably the first of those islanders I've ever seen. Maybe that anyone has ever seen. Who knows what those people would do to get the girl back. Besides that, what would the girl do if she was allowed to stay onboard.

I briefly thought about possibly turning the ship around and taking her back to the island because she seemed like much more trouble than I needed. That thought quickly vanished because not only is there the risk that these people might assume that me and my crew had taken her instead of her leaving of her own free will, but something about taking her back made that tightness in his stomach that much more intense.

I let out a frustrated grunt before turning off the water and stepping out of the shower. I thought the stream of water would help me clear my mind enough to figure out how to deal with this very strange situation I found myself in, but instead I was more confused now then I was before, so there was no point in wasting water.

I grabbed a towel off the nearby rack on the wall, wrapping it around my waist and walking over to the sink. I used my hand to wipe the steam away from the mirror that sat over the sink and stared at my appearance. I wonder if her bite would turn me into a vampire. Should I expect to wake up tomorrow and have the urge to rip my men to pieces? Looking over myself in the mirror, I tried to see if I could notice any changes.

What do blood suckers normally look like? Red eyes? Big fangs? Maybe pale skin? No, besides the fangs, it didn't look like she had any of that. Turning my head from side to side, I studied every inch of my appearance. That's when I saw it. Right in that small patch of skin where my neck met my shoulder. Right where her lips had been just a short while ago was a strange marking.

Not a tattoo but more like a brand burned into my skin. It started in the middle but worked its way outward like one oddly shaped swirl. I ran my fingers across the mark and felt the ridges of it.

Yup, it was real. For a second, I was hoping I was seeing things, but I guess after the day I've had that was too much to ask for.

Chapter 5

I pulled my knees closer to my chest trying to make myself as small as possible in the tiny corner of this bedroom I found myself in. The events of the last hour playing over and over in my head. I bit someone. I bit someone and I enjoyed every minute of it. Why had I gone this long without ever experiencing that?

At home I was never interested in biting someone, I preferred drinking blood from a bottle. Their just seemed to be something so intimate about drinking the blood right from the human's neck. My parents had always had certain stipulations about whose blood I could drink, mostly that it had to be someone they chose, and made it very clear that there would be repercussions for biting someone without their permission. Since I wasn't interested in the act anyway, I had settled for the bottled stuff. Now that I think about it, that was probably just another way for them to control me.

I thought back to the other night at the party, Laurel. The man my parents expected me to marry. Or at least one of the men my parents expected me to marry.

Did they expect me to drink from him? Is that why I was never allowed off the island? Too paranoid that I'd ruin whatever plans they had for me by sucking dry the first human I saw. Well, I guess they weren't wrong because that's exactly what I almost just did. My mind was running a mile a minute as one conspiracy after the other played out in my head about why my parents treated me the way they did. Why they kept me so secluded from the others and my every move was closely monitored. Did they think I would be some uncontrollable monster that would just go around sucking every human dry? I was their daughter, and I was sure they had the same urges I did, that made them just as uncontrollable right?

They weren't always like this. A long time ago, they were completely different people, but then one day -. I lost my train of thought when the bedroom door flew open. An angry Kai wearing nothing but a bath towel wrapped around his waist, barged into the room. The sun was starting to rise, so the thin sunrays shone through the boat windows casting a glow on Kai.

My eyes strayed from the angry expression on his face to the well-defined muscles in his chest. Muscles that were still wet from his shower. My eyes followed one droplet of water as it ran from the dip in his neck, between the outline of his chest muscles and then down the valley of his stomach until it disappeared in the hem of his towel. My throat was suddenly very dry as I remember a short while ago, this man had been beneath me making me feel things I never have before.

"What the hell is this?" His voice jolted me out of the trance I was in. When I looked back at his face, I saw he was tilting his neck to the side. From my position on the floor, it looked like there was a small cut on his neck. Maybe I didn't close the wound all the way after I was done feeding?

"It's just a small scratch." I gave him a small shrug. Call it being stubborn, but I didn't want him to know I felt guilty about what happened. When I tried to apologize before, he snapped at me and called me a freak of nature. Though I guess technically he was right, that doesn't mean it hurt any less to hear him say it.

He let out a frustrated huff before using his long legs to eat up the distance between him and I. He grabbed me by my arms and snatched me from the floor, pulling me close. The force of the pull caused me to slam into his bare chest. I could feel the warm hard muscled beneath my palms.

I had this strong urge to kiss this smooth, tan skin. What is wrong with me? The first man I feed from and now all I could think of was having him beneath me again, or me beneath him.

"Does this look like a small scratch to you?" He jerked my arm out of anger. To a human it might've hurt, but to me all it did was help me pull my mind away from his body and focus on his words.

I pulled my gaze away from his chest and looked at his neck. The moment I did, the lightheadedness I felt before was suddenly back. My heart kicked into overdrive. What did I do?

This girl had been a mystery from the moment she stepped foot on my ship. Not only did I not know her name, but I didn't know what she was running from or where she was running to. One thing I had managed to uncover was the ability to tell when she was lying. Which wasn't hard, she was honestly just bad at it.

When she looked up at me with a horrified, pale expression right before trying to throw on a mask of indifference, I knew anything that came out of her mouth next was going to be a huge lie.

"Looks like a brand." She said as she yanked free of my grip and turned her back to me. "Is that something you sailors normally do?" Yeah, that's exactly what I thought she would do, play clueless, which means whatever this was, was going to be so much worse than I thought it was.

"You really expect me to believe you didn't do this?" I tried to keep the accusing tone out of my voice. I needed answers from her and attacking her wasn't going to be the way I got them.

"Believe what you want to believe. *Freaks of nature* tend to lie." Even with her back to me, the tone in her voice sounded far from angry. More like she was hurt by what I said. Could anyone really blame me, she might look like an innocent young girl, but she was what horror stories were made from. She drank blood, was beautiful, looked incredibly young to speak the way she does and came from a mysterious island where no one leaves.

She was a vampire, by definition, *freak of nature* and until I figured out what she'd done to me she was also dangerous. She walked over towards the small leather couch and grabbed her backpack that sat on top. She threw it over her shoulder before trying to make her way to the door. The moment she tried to brush past me, I stepped in front of her and grabbed her arm.

She's proven time and time again that she was much stronger than she looked so restraining her wasn't something I could do but making her only options hurting me or leaving might be the next best thing. For some reason I had this strange feeling that I could trust that she wouldn't hurt me. "Where do you think you're going?" I asked, tightening my grip on her arm.

"What a stupid question." She held her chin up, trying to give the appearance of confidence, but all it did was make her look like a defiant child, who was in desperate need of punishment.

Punishment. The word was like a straight shot to the cock. It brough back images of her on top of me, riding me like a well-versed champion, which I suspected she wasn't. I tried to push those thoughts deep down. I couldn't think about her like that especially when I was pretty sure what I'm thinking and what we did is illegal.

"I'm leaving. You said you want me off your boat so I'm giving you what you want."

"First, it's a ship not a boat and second, what's your plan, to swim to the next port?" We were in the middle of the ocean with at least a day and a half left of travel. Did she really think she could make it safely to shore? Maybe she could, what the hell did I know.

Her eyes grew wide, and she looked around almost like she had forgotten we were in the middle of a large body of water. That seemed to let the wind out of her sails, and I watched her shoulders slump before she brought her eyes back to mine.

"So, you're going to hold me prisoner here?" The indifferent look remained on her face, but I could see small signs of it slipping. The way her arm shook so slightly in my hold that if I wasn't strangely aware of every move she made, I might have missed it. The little quiver in her voice at the end of her question. I noticed everything and the way she was behaving told me there was a slight chance that she might be more afraid of my crew and I then we should be of her.

I let go of her arm and took a step back, putting some distance between us. "Just to clarify, you hopped aboard my ship, we didn't kidnap you. So, to answer your question, no you're not being held prisoner but there's no way off until we get to the next port, so you're stuck until then."

She sighed and dropped her bag, letting it hang from her fingertips before it ultimately fell to the ground with a thump. "In the meantime, I need some answers from you. It's the least you can do since you've made me an involuntary aid in your grand escape plan from wherever." I waved my arm around emphasizing I wasn't completely clear on where she came from. I had my suspicions, but since she was already in flight-mode, I thought it would be better if I let her tell me. If she was really on the run, asking too many questions would only make her close off more.

"I already told you; I don't know what that mark is." She was still lying. I would find out the truth eventually, so I'll let her off the hook about it for now.

"Fine." I folded my arms across my chest, causing the muscles there and in my arms to flex. I watched as her eyes drifted to the action. Something about the look in her eyes made me very aware that I was still only in a towel and nothing else. Clearing my throat, I continued. "How about we start with something simpler, like a name."

She eyed me suspiciously. "Why do you need that?" she asked.

"I can't keep calling you *the stowaway* now can I." There was a long pause where she just kept looking at me without speaking. I almost thought she just wasn't going to tell me, but then finally she said, "Nicole. My name is Nicole."

Another lie. "Fine, Nicole it is." I turned my back to her and headed over to the small trunk in the corner of the room. I dug through it until I found a white t- shirt and a pair of black sweats. I was tired of standing in a slightly drafty room with nothing but a towel on. It was hard to hold a conversation when I kept wondering what part of my body her eyes would travel to next.

Shaking out the sweatpants, I slipped them on underneath my towel, not even bothering to look for underwear. I could feel her eyes on me as I worked the pants up and over my hips. "So, *Nicole*, why did you hop my ship?"

"I just needed a ride, that's all." When I looked up, I saw her picking at her nails like she didn't have a care in the world.

"How much longer are you going to keep up with this *you don't care* attitude. I'm not buying it so it's not doing you any favors." I slipped the shirt over my head and tossed the used towel onto the bed. When I looked up at her, for just a moment,

I could've sworn I saw a look of disappointment. So, she was enjoying my body just as much as I thought she was. Good to know, but now wasn't the time for that.

I put my hands on my hips. I was getting increasingly bored with this little game she was playing. I said I wouldn't push her, but my patience was running very thin.

"I don't know what you're talking about." I closed my eyes and took a deep breath.

"Let's try this again, why did you hop on my ship?"

"I already to-" It all happened so fast; it shocked the both of us. One second, I was halfway across the room trying to hold my composure at her irritating lies. The next I stood pressing her against the wall one hand holding both her wrists above her head.

She stared at me with wide eyes, mouth hanging open. I was pretty sure my expression mirrored hers. For a long while, neither of us spoke. We just stood frozen, unable to understand what had just happened. It wasn't until I saw her wince that I realized that I still had a tight grip on her wrists. I let go immediately and watched as purple rings began to form around her wrists.

I stared down at my hands, expecting to see some drastic change in them. Maybe I grew claws, or maybe they were twice the size they normally were, anything to explain what just happened. Before, she had proven to be stronger than me. Time and time again she had managed to break free of any hold I had on her. This time though, I had managed to hurt her. That thought made me sick to my stomach.

"What is this?" I asked not taking my eyes off my hands.

"I-I don't know." Her voice trembled and my eyes darted to her face. That pale look had returned to her face, and she stared at my hands unable to pull her eyes away.

I put my hands down by my side but didn't make a move to distance myself from her. "I want answers and I want them now or I swear I'll turn this ship around and drop you back off on that creepy island you call home *Nicole*." I emphasized her name just to make sure she understood that I knew nothing she had told me since she got caught hiding on my ship, was true. Not her name, who she was, why she was on my ship and most of all, what she did to me.

Judging by what just happened, I couldn't deny the possibility that her biting me might've changed me into what she was anymore, but I couldn't bring myself to fully admit it until I heard what she had to say. "Please don't do that," she finally spoke and this time she wasn't putting on airs. The wannabe brave girl who felt like she was too good to answer questions, who didn't fear the fact that she was on a ship in the middle of the ocean surrounded by strange men and headed to a strange place. The girl who did those things to me without thinking about the consequences, who thought lying, very badly if I might add, was the easiest way out of this situation.

All that was left was a scared young girl who was clearly in way over her head. "I can't go back."

"Why not? What are you running from?" She let out a shaky sigh before running her hand through her dark curls. I could still see the angry marks on her wrist, making a tight knot form in my stomach. I ignored it so I could instead focus on what she had to say.

"My father." Was her only response.

"What about him?" I tried to put my emotions in check and not jump to any conclusions. I didn't want to assume this was the average story of a young girl rebelling against her strict father and thought that running away was the best way to get what she wanted. Or maybe that she was running away from some kind of parental abuse.

She took a deep breath before the words spilled from her mouth. Her real name, Niyla. It fit her. I liked it. She told me about how her family shared the same customs as someone from the 1700s, where they thought arranged marriages were okay. How her father wanted her to marry one of the creepy old men that circled her family like vultures and wanted to share in the family power. After months of begging and pleading, she had finally managed to convince said parents to let her have a year of freedom from the island. No supervision, no rules, she could do whatever she wanted. Somehow, out of the entire story, that was the part that sounded the most unbelievable.

The story was so unbelievable, that if it wasn't for this gnawing feeling in the pit of my stomach telling me to believe every word of it, I wouldn't. "This story you've told me about running away from home because of what your father planned to do, I'll believe it, but what you haven't told me is where your plans for this little adventure would lead to."

"I told you; to get away from my father. I won't go back." I sat down on the edge of the bed and threaded my fingers together, leaning forward slightly. The fact that she didn't understand my question told me she was much more naïve than I originally thought.

"You've gotten away from him. You snuck out hopped onto my ship and managed to make a two-day journey on it without anybody noticing you. You're miles away from home where no one can easily get to you, now what?" She still stared at me confused, so I thought it was best to elaborate. "What happens when we finally dock, and you get off the ship? Where are you going to go?"

Recognition shone on her face, and she began pacing the room back and forth. She rubbed her hands together and kept her eyes trained on the floor like it was going to give her the answers she was looking for. "I can always just stick to the original plan I had. My father told me he had gotten me an apartment that's in my name for the next year. If I could just get there, then-" That was the point I knew she was way too naïve and I had to cut her off.

"Where is this apartment?" I asked. She stopped her pacing to stare at me. "That's what I thought." She had no idea any of the important information she needed to know. She let someone else take care of all the details of this supposed year of freedom and up until now, it hadn't crossed her mind that, that would mean her parents would still be able to control everything she did.

"Even if you had any idea where it was, you don't think that will be the first place your father looks for you." Her eyes darted back and forth as she thought about it, then I watched her shoulders slump. She knew I was right. Any plans she had before she left, couldn't be her plans now. Her family would know every move she was going to make, so she would need to come up with something else.

"Well maybe I could-" she started to say, but suddenly she snapped her mouth shut, stopped her pacing, and turned to stare me down. "Why should I tell you my plan? You're telling me to be cautious about everything that could lead them to me, how do I know after I'm gone you won't lead them right to me?"

I leaned back on the bed and placing both my hands flat on it. "Valid question, but I don't make it my business to get in the middle of family drama." I gave a small shrug. "I just thought you might need some help coming up with a different plan." This was her choice, she could let me help her come up with something better and maybe I could get some answers to my questions along the way, or she could figure it out on her own and run the risk of being caught and returned to whatever mid-century society she was a part of. There was only one right choice, the one where we both got what we wanted.

Chapter 6

I knew I was in way over my head the moment I couldn't stop myself from sinking my fangs into a random guy's neck. Hell, I think subconsciously I knew I was in over my head when I decided to sneak out in the middle of my own birthday party, but now as old as I am, I was feeling like every bit of a lost child. I clearly wasn't prepared for what it would be like to leave home without the help of my parents. Now not only was I on my own, but I would be looking over my shoulder at every turn for who knows how long.

To make things worse, I've marked someone. A human to top it off. I sat at the large oak table surrounded by a bunch of rambunctious men of all ages. Some grey around their hairlines and their beards and others look fresh from their mother's apron strings. All of them laughing and enjoying their dinner. From across the room, I could see Kai sitting at a separate table by himself, deep in thought. I could probably imagine what had his mind so wrapped up, because I was feeling the same way.

Almost as if he could sense me staring, he looked up from his plate of untouched food. I flinched and immediately looked down at my own plate of food. The baked chicken and mashed potatoes stared back at me, taunting me. Vampires were allowed to eat normal human food, but after so recently feeding, I didn't have much of an appetite for anything other than Kai's blood. Blood that I could still even now taste on my tongue.

I had marked him. Accidentally, yes, but it doesn't take away from the fact that, that was what I had done. I couldn't bring myself to admit what that meant to him when he asked, but I can admit it to myself. Marking a human means death, for the both of us.

"Girl!" Someone shouted. Seeing as I was apparently the only female aboard this testosterone infested ship, I looked up.

An older man. One with a shaved head, black beard and an eye patch stared me down. Humans didn't scare me, but this man was exactly what children would picture the big bad pirate to look like and the way he was staring at me was making me increasingly uncomfortable.

"Not going to eat, are you?" He asked. I looked down at the food and felt a wave of nausea take over me before I looked back at him and shook my head no. "What's wrong, feeling a little seasick? I guess that's what happens when you stow away on a ship."

I tried to hold my head high to show him that his little comments couldn't intimidate me, but since I was already feeling guilty about everything, including putting everyone on this ship in danger, my efforts to look unphased probably came up a bit short.

A few of the men around him snickered at his comment. What a bunch of children. From the distance I was sitting, I shouldn't have been able to hear anything they were saying, but one of the bonuses of being immortal is the superior hearing that allowed me to enjoy all their invasive questions. I heard one of them even ask if they though Kai had screwed me yet. What lovely language these men had picked up from life at sea.

"Hey girl" The old man spoke up again. "You came from that island of monsters, didn't you?" The men laughed some more. The one sitting next to me even went as far as playfully nudging me in the ribs. I curled my hands into fists so tight, my knuckles began to turn white.

My family and I are not monsters and we didn't deserve to be talked about that way. With every rude comment about my family and I, my control began to slip. A pressure began to build in my head and my jaw began to ache from the effort it took to keep my fangs from descending.

"I heard some of them walk around on all fours and attack anybody that comes to shore. That's not human." That was it, the last little bit of control I had snapped but before I could get to my feet someone spoke up.

"That's enough." I felt a hand slip onto my shoulder, giving me a reassuring squeeze. I looked up to see Kai standing over me. He stared at the old man with irritation clear on his face. In fact, from this angle I was sure I could see the vein in the side of his neck throbbing. I licked my lips as the hunger was slowly beginning to take over. This wasn't the hunger for his blood, no this was the same hunger from before when I wanted nothing more than to touch him.

I wanted to see what his bare skin felt like underneath my hands. I wanted him to touch me just like he did when we were in his bed. He was stronger now because of the mark and I wanted to feel that strength. After the initial shock of his improved speed and strength, I felt nothing but thrill when he had me pinned against the wall. It made me crave a repeat. I wonder what it would take. Would I need to make him angry again?

"Cliff, that's no way to treat our guest now, is it?" Kai said to the old man.

Cliff blew out a puff of air and waved off Kai's comment. "She's not a guest, she's trespassing." He folded his arms across his chest. "Are you going to ignore that fact just because you think she has a pretty face?" Kai's grip on my shoulder tightened.

"Watch what you say next Cliff, or you'll end up just like Julian."

Cliff chuckled, not feeling the least bit threatened by Kai's warning. "Come now *Captain*. It hasn't been that long since you've wet your whistle. At least not long enough for you to want the comfort of any sea witch you come across."

This time no one had a chance to laugh at his disgusting comments because before any of us knew what was happening, Kai had lifted his shirt revealing a leather belt with a matching pouch wrapped around his waist. Inside it sat a small blade with a thick silver and black hilt, a bright blue band tied around it. Kai took the knife out and flung it across the room. It landed on the wood paneling right above Cliff's head.

Several of the crew men around us gasped at the action, but not Cliff. He didn't seem too phased by what happened. In fact, I don't think he moved at all, he just sat there with that unimpressed look on his face, arms still folded. It was almost like he was used to this.

"I told you to watch what you say." As angry as Kai had been with me earlier, I think this is the first time I've heard his voice quite so menacing. Did it sound like that because he was defending me?

"Captain or not," Cliff spoke up, getting to his feet. "You don't command me, boy." He took one final look at me before disappearing through the doorway that led out into the corridor.

Once he was gone, it seemed like the intense atmosphere had completely disappeared. The crew went back to laughing and enjoying their meal, but this time there was no conversation where I was the topic.

Kai disappeared from behind me and took his solitary seat back at his table, leaving me to continue my stare down with the mashed potatoes on my plate. When I looked toward the table Kai sat at, part of me wanted to pick up my plate and go sit with him but another part just kept thinking what if he didn't want me to. So far since I've been on this ship, I've gotten one crew member thrown off, bitten, marked, and lied to another, and caused an argument. I'm really on a roll.

I've only brought him bad luck so far. If I was him, I wouldn't want to be near me either. That thought made me keep my feet planted.

"How long are you planning on staring at those potatoes like they're going to get up and walk away?" I heard the whispered tone of Kai as he leaned down by my ear. I didn't have to look up to know it was him. Even after such a short period of time together, I feel like I could recognize his voice anywhere. Maybe it was the connection from the mark.

"I'm not hungry." I didn't take my eyes off the plate. At the moment, I was having a hard time looking him in the eyes.

Kai walked around me, pulling out the chair to my right and sitting down. I was so lost in thought, I hadn't even realized everyone else had already finished their meals and left the dining hall, leaving me sitting all alone.

"I wonder why." I could hear the sarcasm in Kai's voice, but I chose to ignore it.

I waited for him to get up and leave since I made it very clear I was going to respond, but when he didn't move, I let out the breath I had no idea I was holding in. That was a mistake. The moment I inhaled; I took in his delicious scent. Damn, why did he have to smell that way? Why did I still want more of him when I just so recently fed?

"You don't have to sit here and wait for me to finish. I'm sure I can find my way back once I'm done." Kai still didn't move. I could feel his eyes burning into the side of my head, but something told me looking him in the eyes right now wouldn't be the best idea. It was so hard to just sit there while he stared, it made me feel like a science experiment on display for everyone to gawk at. It was bad enough I had to deal with one of his crew members hurling insults at me, now I had to sit here while he *examined* me to his heart's content, trying his hardest to see all the things I was keeping from him.

My leg began shaking the longer we sat there in silence. I needed something to do with my hands, so I picked up my fork and began absentmindedly pushing the mashed potatoes back and forth across my plate. I was just about to snap and tell him I was done eating when he beat me to it and spoke first. "How long do you expect me to go along with this lie you told me about this mysterious mark on my neck?" My head snapped in his direction. I guess I shouldn't underestimate the stubbornness of a human.

"How long are you going to insist on having the same conversation. I told you I don't know what it is." I half expected him to leave the topic alone, but part of me knew he wouldn't and since I still couldn't bring myself to tell him the truth and cause further disruption to his life, I had decided to keep the same lie going. With that being said, the anxious feeling I was having because of the way he was staring at me mixed with the guilt gnawing at the pit of my stomach, made the lie that spilled past my lips not so convincing.

My voice cracked, the moment the words *I don't* came out of my mouth. This wasn't just a subtle squawk that only I would notice, but a very obvious noise that caused Kai's eyes to zero in on my mouth. He smirked at me when he lifted his eyes to meet mine. He knew I was lying and now he would never let this go.

"The way I see it, you're stuck on this ship for the next couple of days. When we dock, you have absolutely no idea where you're going or who you can trust not to turn you in." I clenched my teeth. We both knew he was right. I was on my own in a world I knew nothing about. I didn't have any money nor a place to stay and as it has so recently been proven to me no clue how to hunt undetected. If we were to arrive at the next stop tomorrow and I was left to my own devices I'd been caught immediately and depending on who did the catching, human or vampire, I'd be killed because of what I am.

Even knowing all of this already, it didn't feel great to have him throwing it in my face at every turn. Like he was calling me foolish for leaving without a better plan. He could never understand how much of a risk it was to leave or what an even greater danger it would've been to stay. How could he, he's just a simple human who captains a simple ship and lives a simple life. At least that was the case before I showed up.

"Get to the point already." I looked anywhere but his face. The wall behind his head where the knife still stuck out from the wall was a great option. "What do you want?"

Kai lifted his hand up and grabbed my chin, adjusting so I was forced to look at him. "I told you what I want." That stupid smirk returned to his face. "I want to know everything. You want to know all my secrets of survival; I want to know all of yours."

"I told you everything."

"I don't think you have and now with the right incentive, maybe you will." This poor human. Here I am trying to look out for his well-being when he has been nothing but a pest to me since I boarded this ship. Not only did I feel guilty about what I had done, but I also thought that it would be safer if I just left the ship and him behind without him knowing the truth behind the mark I had left on his neck.

I didn't want him to feel responsible for me. Hell, I didn't even know if he would care enough to feel that way, but now he was using this as a levering tool so that I had no choice but to tell him. Fine, if that's what he wanted, I would tell him everything.

"You're right, I did lie. You want to know the truth?" That smirk turned into a full-blown smile as he let go of my chin and sat back in his chair, never taking his eyes off me. I took a deep breath and let the words fly. "You've been marked."

Chapter 7

I had once again found myself sitting on the edge of Kai's bed while he paced back and forth in front of me looking every bit as if his head was about to explode. In all fairness I did try to keep the truth from him and if he wasn't being such an annoying pest, that's where the truth would've stayed.

"So let me get this straight..." He tried for the third time to ask a question and for the third time he had stopped midway through. I told him everything. Ok, *almost* everything. Only the things I knew to be facts and not things that were rumored to be true and even then, only the things I thought he absolutely needed to know.

He knew what was required for someone to be marked. That it had to be done during a mating, or in our case something close to a mating. I had to take his blood when the two of us reach our peaks. That is how it went between two vampires anyway. I didn't know all the rules behind marking a human, so I was at a loss. If Kai never took my blood, how was the mark formed? And if we were now bonded, was it the same as for two vampires, the only way to put an end toward this connection is with the death of one of us.

The things that fell under the category of *best kept to myself* were as follows, I had no idea why his mark looked completely different from the marks I had seen in the books back home. Honestly, I had only heard rumors of an immortal marking a human years ago, so this was all completely new to me. The most important thing I decided to keep to myself was what would happen to me once I got off this ship. That was something I would have to worry about though, not him.

Kai opened his mouth to try again. "So, in your world, this is like marriage?" I wanted to laugh at the question. Of course, that's what he would be wondering about. A strange girl shows up hiding on his ship, one who preferred to keep as much about herself and her life private, and now he was thought to be married to her.

"In my world." I repeated the words back to him, making sure I emphasized my world. "Yes, this would be considered a marriage."

Kai stopped his pacing so he could look at me. His face a little bit paler then no normal, then again it could be the crappy lighting provided by this old ship he seemed so fond of. "Am I turning into one of you?" He asked.

I shook my head. Marking someone and turning them were only slightly different, but I didn't feel like now was the time to explain that to him. It seemed more like he wanted reassurance that he wasn't turning into a monster like me. When I shook my head no, the relief he felt was evident in the way his shoulders dropped a little, but I could still tell that this was a lot of information for one little human to take in at a time. This is why my kind tended to keep our identities and the truth about us a secret.

"Can it be removed?" He asked.

I tried not to show the slight sting I was feeling at how desperate he was to hear the answer to that question, but I guess that would be considered a reasonable reaction to someone not accustomed to something like this. In my world, this was normal, it happened almost every day, but Kai wasn't from my world. I sighed and suddenly the ponytail that sat high on my head was way too tight. I lifted my arms up and tugged trying to loosen it at least a little. "No, marks are permanent."

His head and shoulders dropped, and he let out a sigh before he began pacing again. I didn't like how his look of disappointment made me feel so I looked away and instead kept my eyes focused on my hands. "So, what do we do now?" He asked.

"There's only one thing to do," He looked up, hope in his eyes that maybe I had found a solution. "I get off this ship at the next port and we never see each other again." The hope changed to confusion as he tried to process what I said.

"What does that mean? You just said the mark can't be removed and the only way to break the connection is if one of us dies so what happens to the connection if we never see each other again?" I die. That's what happens if we separate permanently. Now that I've marked him, I can't drink the blood from any other human and regular food would only sustain me for so long. The inevitable is that I would starve. That was one of the rumors I had heard about a bond between an immortal and a human. I no longer needed confirmation, ever since I had taken his blood the scent of every other human on this ship has made me almost physically sick. I don't think that's a coincidence.

I wasn't Kai's problem. I'm the one that stowed away on his ship, and then attacked him. I wasn't going to disrupt his life anymore then I already have. If I had never left that night neither of us would be in the situation, we were in. Since this was my fault, I would make sure we could both get our freedom even if mine was only for a short time, it was better than nothing at all. "You won't feel it as much if I'm not around." Another lie. "Eventually it'll fade until it's almost nonexistent." I hope.

He looked at me like he wasn't sure if he should really believe the things, I was telling him, but eventually he nodded. Kai crossed the room, heading for the door and for a second I thought he was going to leave. If he did then I could finally loosen the tight grip, I had on the bed sheets. Being in this enclosed space with his scent was driving me crazy, I could barely think straight.

I guess today just wasn't going to be my lucky day because instead of him leaving the room like I thought, he flicked the light switch causing the whole room to be surrounded in darkness except for the small window that allowed moonlight in. Then if that wasn't bad enough, he grabbed the edges of his black t-shirt and pulled it up over his head. I sat there staring wide eyed at him. He however seemed completely unphased by the situation and instead sat on the edge of the bed kicking off his boots and laying back in the bed.

I finally found enough of my voice to ask, "What are you doing?"

He slipped his arms behind his head and closed his eyes. "Sleeping what does it look like?"

"You're sleeping here?"

He opened his eyes to look at me in amusement. "This is my room, where else would I sleep?"

He couldn't mean that we would sleep together, so I guess that meant he wanted me to find somewhere else to go for the night. I got to my feet and turned to face him. "Right, I guess I'll see you in the morning."

Just as I was turning to head toward the door, Kai sat up and grabbed my wrist, yanking my arm and making me lose my balance. I gasped as I landed right on top of him, my legs on either side of his hips and my hand landing right on his smooth, hard bare chest. "Where are you going?" He asked.

I lifted my head a little so I could look at him and it was at that moment I realized how close we were. His big blue eyes, staring at me, stole my breath and his lips were so close to mine. If I just moved my head a few centimeters forward, I could taste them again. Maybe if I was rough enough, I could draw blood. My mouth watered when I thought about his blood, and I couldn't help it when my tongue shot out to lick my lips. This action brough Kai's full attention to my mouth and the way his eyes darkened slightly, I had a feeling he was having the same thoughts as me. Maybe not about the blood but the intense urge to close the distance between us.

Kai reached up with his free hands and grabbed my chin, pulling it towards him until our lips touched. Smooth, soft, and sure. My experience with kissing was limited to a few servants I would play around with over the centuries when I was bored, but I knew enough to pass judgement that Kai was a very skilled kisser. He knew just what to do to make me see fireworks behind my eyelids and make that heat build in my lower belly and between my legs. The way he turned his head slightly to deepen the kiss and nibbled on my bottom lip until I opened for his sweet tongue. When his tongue met mine, I couldn't help the contented sigh that escaped me. It felt good. Really good.

I heard a slight rumble come from Kai's chest and then he slipped his arm around my waist, pulling me closer. I had a sense of déjà vu when I felt his hard length pressing against my center. I didn't want it to be like before, this time I wanted to be closer. I wanted to feel more of his skin on mine, but we were both wearing way too many clothes. Kai must've been thinking the same thing because he broke the kiss just long enough to grab the edges of my shirt and pull it up over my head, then before I knew what was happening, he had flipped our positions so I was the one laying on my back and he hovered over me, looking at me the same way a lion would a gazelle.

He leaned in and lightly brushed his lips against my neck, sending a shiver down my spine before he dove in sucking hard on the spot where my neck and shoulder meant. I wrapped my arms around his neck, pulling him closer and arching my back so I pressed my body closer to him. Why did he feel so good, smell so good, taste so good. I wanted to be closer. I shouldn't be the only one feeling good. I wanted to give him to feel this good too.

I slid one hand down his side until I reached his hip. I tried to slip my hand in between our bodies so I could reach the buttons on the front of his pants, but there wasn't enough space. He was both too close but not close enough. Kai tightened his grip on my waist and shifted his position, rotating us so he was the one lying flat on his back, and I was back to straddling his hips.

I sat there momentarily dazed, both our chests heaving as we tried to catch our breath. I swallowed trying to moisten my dry mouth and let my eyes wonder down his bare chest, enjoying the view. My eyes zeroed in on the button that was out of reach before but was ripe for the picking now.

I leaned forward and popped the button open, eager to see more of him, but before I could reveal more of his flesh he grabbed my wrist, stilling my movements. My eyes shot up to meet his. "Don't start something you're not ready to finish." It wasn't a demand. The way he was looking at me, it almost seemed like he was begging me not to change my mind. We were on the same page; I couldn't change my mind about this even if I wanted to. Right now, I couldn't form any other thought besides what we were doing right now.

I reached for the button again and this time he let me have my way. With one quick flick of my fingers the button popped open, and I was meant with the view of the black band of his boxer briefs. I grabbed the edges of his jeans and tried sliding them down. He lifted slightly so I could get them down past his thighs. I reached for his briefs next and within minutes those were down as well. As I stood face to face with his cock,

I realized, I had no idea what to do next. Secretly experimenting with some of the male servants back home was nothing compared to the things Kai, and I had done together, just a little touching here and there. Hell in the short amount of time that we've known each other, he'd already managed to do what those other guys couldn't and that was give me my first orgasm and we were still fully clothed. It's safe to say it was well worth the wait though.

Have I ever held a man in my hands before? Yes, but with Kai this all felt different, new. I wanted to do more, try harder. With him, I wanted to put my mouth on him. I licked my lips which suddenly felt dry as that thought crossed my mind. Most men liked when women used their mouths right? I guess the obvious question was would I be able to do a good job?

"Do you want to stop?" Kai's question pulled me from my thoughts. I hadn't realized I'd been staring until he said something. I glanced at him and could see the concern written all over his face. It was sweet that he was worried about my comfort at this moment, but he didn't need to be, after everything I had put him though in such a short amount of time, it was the least I could do, not to mention I had this strange feeling that doing this would give me an incredible amount of satisfaction.

I shook my head no and slid down his body, so I was straddling his calves and his cock was angled right at my mouth. Licking my lips one final time, I leaned forward and opened as wide as I could. Just because I lived on an island practically cut off from civilization doesn't mean I didn't have my methods of gaining access to a few helpful sources of information. I knew one day my curiosity would pay off; thank God I didn't have to test out what I learned on that stupid werewolf wannabe my father had lined up for me.

The first contact my lips made with him caused his whole body to twitch and my body mirrored his reaction. It was a very strange thing to have his manhood between my lips. The skin was so smooth and soft, yet I could feel the hard muscle underneath begging for release. He tasted sweet which was strange, everything I'd read about the taste said I should expect a salty or bitter taste but not Kai, he was perfect. Was this part of the bond or was this how he always tasted?

He groaned when I pursed my lips slightly, creating a tighter fit. I could feel his hips raise off the bed slightly, pushing himself further into my mouth. I wrapped one hand around the base of his member, gripping snuggly and began bobbing my head up and down at the same time, I twisted my wrist back and forth. I couldn't take as much of him inside as I wanted to, so I decided to make up for it by increasing the speed. I continued to increase my speed until I had a nice rhythm going and I was rewarded with Kai reaching down and placing his hand on my head. It started as a light touch but quickly changed to him tugging on the hair tie in my head, pulling it loose so he could run his fingers through my hair and message my scalp. His touch was soothing but was fanning the flames of my own arousal. I wanted more but I was determined to get him to finish first.

Kai's hips began moving fast in time with the way I moved my head up and down on him. We were so in sync, every time he dropped his hips pulling from my mouth, my head followed keeping him as submerged as I could, never giving him time to catch his breath. His moans got louder so much so that I was worried the whole ship would hear him, but it was obvious he didn't care one bit.

"Oh fuck, I'm so close." He groaned again so I increased my speed more.

"Cap! You busy?" Someone called from the other side of the bedroom door followed by a knock. I stilled instantly the small growl of irritation that came from Kai took me completely by surprise. He slipped from my mouth, and I made a move to get off him, but he grabbed my wrist stopping me. When I looked at his face, he held up his finger to his lips telling me to keep my voice down.

"Cap! You sleep in there?" The voice called again. I held my breath when I heard the doorknob jiggle slightly but didn't budge. I had never been so grateful for the invention of locks before in my life.

After what seemed like the longest minute and a half in the history of time, I finally heard footsteps of the crewman moving further and further away from the door. I let out a sigh of relief and let my shoulders slump a little. I was so grateful not to be caught in this compromising position.

Kai broke the silence before I could. "Well, that could've been awkward."

Chapter 8

Avoidance was key in making sure nothing like what happened a few days ago would happen again. I had to be stuck on this ship until the next port, but that didn't mean I had to stay close to Kai. During the day I explored the ship, it was huge and from the looks of it they transported a lot of different goods for different parts of the world. I've seen different types of food and grain, mechanical parts, I've even seen a few different livestock like chickens and goats. If I had the chance, I would've loved to see all the different places this ship had seen. Maybe in another life under different circumstances that would've been possible.

At night, I knew Kai expected me to share his bed so we could finish what keeps getting interrupted, but that was no longer an option. I can't drink from him anymore and the longer I'm around him the harder it was from me to control that urge. I also couldn't deny the fact that every time I was around him, it seemed to be harder and harder from me when it was time for us to separate. I guess that was the effects of the mark. I felt like I was becoming dependent on his presence and if I wanted to keep myself from feeding from him, that couldn't happen. We would arrive at the port later today, all I needed was to hold out until then and then I could disappear, and he would be safe.

I sat with my legs dangling over the edge of the front of the boat, looking out at the clear span of ocean water. You couldn't see land yet, but I knew it wouldn't be long before I could see the dark line beginning to form on the horizon.

"You know you really shouldn't sit on the edge like that." The hairs on the back of my neck stood on end when I heard that voice. Whenever he was around, it seemed like all the nerves in my body vibrated and I couldn't get them to stop. Once I'm away from him, hopefully that would all change. I took a deep breath before turning to face him. That fitted black button up with the sleeves rolled up leaving his bulging biceps on full display, was enough to make my heart skip a beat. The buttons carelessly left open all the way down to the center of his chest leaving those beautiful collar bones on full display and making my mouth water for a taste.

"You're making the rest of the crew nervous like that you know."

I gave a little shrug and turned back to face the water. It was best I avoided looking at him as much as I could. "That's nothing different from the usual. They already think I'm the monster from the mysterious island, maybe they're hoping I'll go ahead and jump overboard."

I could hear the small laugh behind me followed by the approaching footsteps. My back stiffened. I really didn't want him any closer but unless I decided to take that joke seriously and jump overboard, there really wasn't anywhere else for me to go. He stood next to me, leaning on the partial metal railing. I didn't look at him, but I could feel him boring holes in the side of my face with those mesmerizing eyes of his.

"I wanted to tell you," He said after a long stretch of silence followed by him clearing his throat. I wonder, did he have the same struggle with focus around me as I did him? "I called in a favor, and I was able to find a place for you to stay for a few days until you can figure out where you want to go."

Where I wanted to go? A few days ago, there was so many places I wanted to visit, maybe even live one day. Then again, a few days ago I hadn't signed my own death certificate. Kai couldn't know that though, he had to think I would go off and live my life so he could do the same. If he found out the truth, I had a feeling he would try to do something about it, and I refuse to derail his life anymore.

When I didn't show my immediate gratitude, he kept talking. "If you still need help coming up with a plan to stay hidden, I'm still willing to help you with that." He took another step towards me. He was so close now I could feel the heat radiating from his body even with the strong, cold breeze coming off the water. "Are you finally willing to tell me why you're running from your family. If I'm going to help, I should at least know what this is about right?"

Kai did have a right to know. I was putting his life in danger, and he didn't even know what this was about. What would he do if I told him the real reason I left home, was to escape an arranged marriage. Would he think I was just some spoiled child that ran away from home? When he finally realized how deep the meaning of the mark was, would he think I did it on a whim or would he believe me when I told him none of this was part of my plan?

If my father ever caught up to me or worse him, he was as good as dead so maybe it was time, I told him what he was really dealing with. "My family. They're not the type to enjoy hearing the word no."

Not a lie, but not the complete truth either. He sighed and placed his hand on the small of my back, making the air rush from my lungs. "That's all you're going to give me, isn't it?" Silence was my answer to his question. "We should be able to see land in an hour and we dock in about four." That was all he said before he pulled his hand away, turned his back to me and left me alone with my thoughts.

Kai was right, I had sat there for the entire hour he promised would reveal land along the horizon. My heart raced when I saw it, but I didn't know why. Was it because when we reached it, I would have to leave Kai's side or because once I was on my own, I would be... on my own? I would have no one to answer to but myself. Every decision would be my own.

It wasn't long before the blaring horn could be heard coming from the top of the ship signaling that we were docking. Kai hadn't come back to speak to me again since telling me he had found somewhere for me to hide out and I guess that was a good thing. I needed to get used to being away from him. I thought these last few days of avoiding him had helped, but the moment he was in my presence, it was like all my hard work had gone straight down the drain.

I pulled my legs back from the edge of the ship and headed back inside to grab my bag. This was it.

I watched as some of the crewmen made their way down the ramp to help the workers on the pier secure the ship so it wouldn't drift away. I took a deep breath, picked up my bag that was sitting on the edge of the ship right next to me, and began heading toward the ramp. That's what I thought anyway, at least until I felt a strong hand on my arm yanking me back and pulling me behind the stacked crates that hadn't been unloaded yet.

I looked up and came face to face with those eyes that were becoming increasingly difficult to ignore. "What are you doing? I thought you were going to introduce me to the people that were going to hide me."

"Be quiet." Kai whispered, putting his hand over my mouth. He pulled me closer to him, making sure I was hidden from the view of everyone else. "Do you see the guy leaning against the post over there. Black suit. Do you know him?" Kai turned me so my back was pressed firmly against his chest, but he never removed his hand from my mouth.

I tried peeking around the corner of the stacked crates as best I could without being seen. It took me a second to spot the man he was talking about, but the moment I did, it felt like my heart had dropped all the way down to my feet.

I hadn't seen him often, but I never forgot a face. He was one of the guards from home. Which could only mean one thing, my father had found me. The look on my face must've told Kai everything he needed to know. He pulled me back out of view and turned me so I would face him.

"Who is he?" He asked. I didn't speak, just dropped my eyes to look at the ground and shook my head in response. All I could think was that they had found me. They had found me among humans, one of which I had made the mistake of marking. They would kill him and everyone else on this ship. The panic set in quick. As an immortal, one of the strongest creatures to walk this planet, it seemed like I spent most of my existence in a constant state of fear and I was sick of it, but what could I do about it?

While I stood there like a scared little child, Kai immediately jumped into action. "We can't let him see you get off this ship." Kai turned and began heading back to the living quarters, dragging me along with him.

"What are you doing? I must find a way to get past him. I can't just stay on board." I tried tugging my hand away from him, but it seemed with all my effort to stay away from him, the mark had made his strength increase significantly. I had to put in effort to break free. Before I could take a step away from him, he grabbed my hand again.

"It's too late for that. If that guy is anything like you, there is no way you'll make it off this ship without being caught." I chewed on my lip nervously. As much as I hated to admit it, he was right. From what I could see, this town we docked in wasn't that big, there was no where I could hide that they wouldn't find me and so making it off this ship was not only impossible, but also pointless. In other words, I was stuck. They would catch me, and I would be forced back home and kept on an even tighter leash by my father then I was before.

I let Kai drag me the rest of the way until we reached his room. He closed the door behind us, and I plopped down on the bed and let me head fall into my hands. Would I ever be free of this nightmare, or would I have to keep running for the rest of my life and end up taking Kai down with me?

Kai paced back and forth in front of me, every so often scratching his head. He was clearly just as much at a loss as I was. I sat and listened to the workers stomping around overhead as they unloaded their delivery and probably picked up a new load for the next port. It wouldn't be long before they began to wonder where the captain was. They would have questions about why they never saw me leave the ship even though he promised that this was as far as they would take me.

"Ok." He finally said. "I guess we have no choice," I looked up just as Kai turned to face me. "We can't get you safely off at this port without you being seen, so you'll just have to stay on until we get to the final port."

"You're kidding right?" I shot to my feet, folding my arms as I stared him down. I could barely handle being on this stupid ship for as long as I have and now, he wants me to stay on for I don't know how much longer until we get to another port. There was no way I would be able to resist his blood any longer than I had.

"What other choice do we have? Unless you forgot to tell me you also can make yourself invisible, it's either this or you go back with him." I chewed on the inside of my cheek as I stared at him. I could tell he was waiting for further resistance from me, but what could I say really? He was right. My only argument was that I didn't want to be stuck on a ship with him and his sweet-smelling blood any longer and I didn't want him to know that.

"When we get to the final port, you'll stay with me at least until we figure out what to do next."

She didn't voice any other rejections to what I was suggesting, and I was relieved. This strange girl had fought me on everything ever since she got on this ship and even more so after leaving this mark on my neck. I wasn't sure what had changed between that day and now, but I was going to use this extra time I had with her to figure that out.

I watched as she plopped back down on the bed defeated and I couldn't lie to myself, watching how she reacted to having to spend more time with me stung and I didn't know why.

For me, the urge to be around her was almost unbearable. She said that because of what she did to me, we would have this bond, but I didn't think it would be like this. I ache when she isn't near me, but it seemed like the opposite for her. For the last few days, she had gone out of her way to make sure she was anywhere I wasn't.

I let out a sigh and turned my back to her, heading for the door. I had to help the rest of my crew quickly finish up so we could depart as soon as possible. I didn't need that guy deciding he wanted to start snooping around the ship.

"Stay away..." I stopped in my tracks, confusion making my face scrunch up. *"Blood."* I looked around trying to figure out where the voice was coming from before finally turning to face Niyla. There she sat with her eyes still trained to the ground. Maybe I was hearing things. I turned to leave when I heard the voice again, a voice that sounded a lot like hers but as I stared at her I knew it didn't come from her mouth. *"... like Cira."*

I turned to face her completely and took a step towards her. She looked up at me and for a second, it almost looked like she had tears in her eyes but then she blinked, and they were gone.

"Who is Cira?"

Chapter 9

The pale look on Niyla's face told me that maybe I shouldn't have asked that question. It was too late now; I couldn't take the words back and I couldn't deny the fact that, based on her reaction, I was even more curious about this mysterious Cira. I'm not even sure where the name came from.

"Who is-" Before I had a chance to ask again, in a flash I was thrown up against the wall. Niyla's face was inches from mine. Her arm pressed against my throat, holding me in place. I watched as her eyes turned a bright glowing red and her sharp canines extended past her lips. If it wasn't for the angry look on her face the sharp teeth would strangely be a turn on. I remember the way they felt lodged in the side of my neck. Her soft lips on my skin when she pulled blood from my vein. I lost my train of thought when she tightened her hold on my throat.

Even with this enhanced strength thanks to this mark, it was starting to become increasingly difficult to breathe.

"How do you know that name?" She spoke through clenched teeth. I tapped on her arm to let her know it would be easier to speak if I could breathe. It took a minute, but the red in her eyes began to disappear but her fangs remained on full display. "Talk. Are you working for Ezra?" Ezra? Who the hell is Ezra?

"I'm... not... working with anyone." I gasped out and attempted to push her arm away, but she didn't budge.

"Who told you that name?" She tightened her grip again and I made another poor attempt at getting her to release me.

"Nobody." My response came out as nothing more than a whisper.

Her fangs disappeared and her grip finally loosened. "I knew I shouldn't have trusted you." In the blink of an eye, she disappeared, and I was left standing in an empty bedroom.

How? How could he know that name? That name was supposed to be erased from history. Years ago, when Cira disappeared and left me all alone in that place, I said I would never think about her again. She was gone and I was left to deal with my family and the isolation. Why would he know that name?

Had he been playing me this whole time? Was he tasked with keeping me entertained by my father? Just giving me the false sense of freedom before taking me back? Was my marking Kai factored in at all? I couldn't trust anyone that was clear to me now.

I guess I didn't need to question how that guard found me anymore. Kai tipped him off. Was that his plan, to make it so I was forced to stay on the ship until the last port and once we got there, my father would be there waiting to take me back? What did he get out of this though? Money? What was worth him trading my freedom?

I didn't have a plan of what I was going to do. Yes, it was true I couldn't stay with Kai, and I had escaped him, but how was I going to get passed the guard that stood watch on the dock. If I could just blend in with the other workers, I could get pass him without being noticed. I hid behind some crates and watched the workers deal with the cargo. Looking around, I tried spotting the guard, but he wasn't standing against the post on the docks anymore. In fact, he didn't appear to be anywhere. I watched the workers on the dock for a little while longer, but it wasn't until I saw them load the last of the cargo onto the ship and I began to feel the hairs on the back of my neck begin to stand on end that I decided to make my move. Over the last few days, I noticed whenever Kai was around, it was like my body was on high alert, so that meant at this very moment he was looking for me and getting very close. I had to move now while it looked like I had the chance.

In a flash I was gone. I took off running, speeding past the crew members as they were climbing back onboard. They felt nothing but a gust of wind as I moved past them, too quick for their eyes to catch me. I ran and ran, zipping through the small town, not stopping until I found myself at a dead end. Staring at the three stone walls of the alley, I took in my surroundings but there wasn't much to see. Trash littered each wall, an old dumpster overflowing with trash sat in a corner and old clotheslines lined with undergarments hung above my head.

My nose was assaulted by all the horrible smells around me. It smelled of rotten food, cigarette smoke and urine. The one thing I didn't smell, the enticing allure of Kai's blood. Good, that meant I had gotten far enough away from him that he shouldn't be able to track me. If I was lucky, he would think I was still on the ship until after they departed. He would be far at sea before he realized I was left behind.

I took a step further into the alley, pressing my back against the wall, leaning my head back on the cool stone wall and tried to think of my next move. That was becoming increasingly difficult to do because I could feel my stomach begin seizing slightly. This only happened when I hadn't fed for a while and since I hadn't fed from anyone since I fed from Kai, it's been at least 2 or 3 days. For now, I was hoping I could hold off long enough to come up with a plan.

I had never had to hunt before, there were always a few human blood slaves kept in the castle for things like this. It was purely an accident when I attacked Kai. Even with no previous hunting experience, I knew there was no way I could grab someone in broad daylight, so I would have to wait until nightfall and with any luck grab someone when they walked past the alley. Letting out a sigh, I slid down the wall and pulled my knees against my chest until I was crouched in a corner hidden from anyone walking past.

There is nothing left to do now but wait until night fall. That's what I thought anyway until I heard glass breaking followed by some low grumbling. I couldn't see where the noise was coming from with the position I held crouched behind the dumpster, but I could smell it. Strong scents of alcohol and vomit started overpowering all the other scents around me. Another smell that stood out to me, blood. Human blood.

I shifted so I was on my knees and peeked around the dumpster so I could get a better view. I saw a dark shadow standing at the edge of the alley, just out of sight from all the passersby. He stumbled around and I watched him throw a glass bottle to the ground and it shattered. He cursed and brought his hand to his mouth to suck on a few fingers. Fingers, that were bleeding. I could smell it even from this distance. The blood smelled repulsive. Nothing like the sweet smell of Kai's blood, but my hunger was getting the best of me and my mouth began to fill with saliva. I could feel my fangs begin to lengthen at the same time my stomach gave another squeeze.

I was so hungry, and he was right there. All I needed was one little bit. It would be so simple to just grab him. He wouldn't even remember it when he woke up, I would be gone. The pains in my stomach wouldn't be a distraction anymore and then my mind would be clear enough to plan out what I should do next to say out of my father's reach.

I was so busy with my mind running a mile a minute, I hadn't realized that I had changed my position from crouching behind the dumpster to moving in front of the dumpster but staying in the shadows of the alley. He had his back to me and hadn't been alerted to my presence at all, so all I needed to do was take a few more steps and he would be in my reach.

I held out my arm, ready to place it on his shoulder, it was like I was in a trance. A sort of tunnel vision and all I could see was him, so it completely escaped my notice that a large piece of the glass bottle he had dropped early was right in front of me until I kicked it.

The man turned around; his eyes wide when they locked on mine. I wondered in that moment what I looked like to him. The red eyes, the extended fangs, even the sharp claws that were starting to extend out of the ends of my fingers. I wondered if

I looked like the monster I felt like at that moment. I didn't want to drink from him, I hated everything about this process. Even being back home in the house I grew up in with the slaves we kept in the castle, I hated feeding from anyone who was unwilling.

Kai, he was willing. He gave himself to me and I knew he enjoyed it just as much as I did, but I was wonder now, if that was all an act too.

Before the thought could cross his mind to run away from me, my hands were on his shoulders. He gasped when I pushed him against the wall, his body frozen stiff. He didn't scream, he didn't even speak, he just stared at me with wide eyes and a pale expression like he thought this would be the moment I killed him. I wouldn't, I would only take enough to make the pain stop. That was all I needed.

I wasn't sure how long this would ease the pain or if it even would at all. I was bonded with someone already and I wasn't supposed to drink the blood from another. This could potentially kill me, but I had to try something.

I leaned into him and took a deep inhale of his scent. He smelled of sweat, vomit and alcohol, a smell that under normal circumstances would repulse me but I couldn't afford to be picky. I tried focusing on the scent of his blood instead which was hard to do with the other scents almost overpowering it.

"Shh, it won't hurt." I tried soothing him when I felt him begin to squirm. I could stop myself. I know I could. I would not kill this man. "I just need a little bit." He squirmed even more, so I tightened my grip. With one more inhale, I opened my mouth wide and bit down. I felt his body stiffen when I took the first pull on his vein. The taste was horrible, just as rancid as he smelled but thankfully it helped with the seizing in my stomach and that's all I wanted.

I swallowed another mouth full and then another and I didn't stop until I felt him going limp against the wall. I pulled back and I felt my fangs recede. I let out a sigh of relief that it was over. The pain in my stomach had stopped, the fog in my head was gone and even though it was faint, I could hear the man's steady breathing, which meant I hadn't taken too much from him.

I gave one final lick to the side of his neck to catch any extra blood I might've missed and to help seal the wound and then I released him. He slid down the wall and became a crumpled mess on the floor. Leaving him there shouldn't be a problem, anybody who walks by would just think he was passed out drunk, which wasn't too far from the truth.

I guess the rumors that I wouldn't be able to drink anyone else's blood were just that, rumors. I wasn't feeling sick, and I actually felt stronger now than I had in a few days. I stood up, straightened my shoulders, and turned my back to the drunkard, heading out of the alley. I didn't know where I was heading but I knew it was best to keep moving and hope I would come up with a plan along the way.

Stepping out into the bright streets, I looked around at all the people. Couples holding hands and smiling. Mothers pushing their babies in carriages. Even groups of guys in strange shirts with numbers written on them high fiving each other as they entered a large brown building with a picture of what looked like a chicken on it. Everyone here was so happy and carefree. No one was running or hiding from anyone or anything. I wondered for a moment if I could do that too. Be free, happy, and carefree here where nobody would know who or what I was.

It was a nice thought, but there was no way I could stay here. If Kai decided to come and find me this would be the first place, he decided to check, and I couldn't let him find me again. I continued my exploration of the small seaside town, the cute shops and all the people. It wasn't until I turned a corner and caught a whiff of something. I couldn't quite put my finger on what it was, but the moment I smelled it, the rumbling in my stomach returned, but this time in full force.

Unlike before when it was just a slight stabbing, hunger pains, this time I wasn't craving to take something in, this time something wanted to come out. A dizzying feeling overtook me and my vision began to blur. I was barely able to make it to a trash can before I emptied the contents of my stomach into it.

It just kept coming and it didn't seem like it would ever stop. When it was done, and I wiped my mouth, I realized the only thing I was throwing up was blood. The only blood I've had in days was that drunk's.

Suddenly my knees buckled, and I instantly dropped to them. I clutched at my stomach as the rumbling continued. There was nothing left to come up, but I still had the urge to purge something from my body, and I had no idea how to get it to stop.

The pain was unbearable as sweat began to form on my forehead, and it wasn't long before the edges of my vision began to blur. I was blacking out, but I couldn't do it here. There were people after me, I couldn't just pass out on the streets of a town I wasn't familiar with. Who knew where that guard was, he could be close by right now just waiting for a moment I was vulnerable so he could grab me and take me back to my father.

I had to hide. I lifted myself up on my elbows and tried to drag my suddenly, incredibly heavy body as far as I could. I could just barely see a small dark doorway. If I could just make it there, I would be safe. Slowly I inched forward, but every time it seemed like I was getting just a little closer, the doorway seemed to move further away.

All the air seemed to have left my lungs, I couldn't go on anymore. My vision darkened more and that was it. I couldn't move anymore. My body collapsed and the last thing I saw before everything went completely black was a pair of feet stepping in front of me.

<h1 style="text-align:center">Chapter 10</h1>

I wasn't sure how long I had been out of it. All I knew was that when I came to, the pain in my stomach had lessened but was still very noticeable. It was a struggle to even open my eyes, they felt like they were being held closed by huge, heavy weights. I groaned and rolled to my side, clutching at my stomach. Attempting again to pry open my eyes, I managed to open them enough to get a slight peek at my surroundings and I saw powder blue walls with big white splotches on them. It reminded me of a clear blue sky. I turned a little more and I saw the two large white windows that let large amounts of sunlight flood the room, making everything almost glow. It made my already sensitive eyes hurt even more.

I jerked up to a sitting position, trying to take in more of my surroundings but I didn't recognize anything. Jerking my body like that I realized was a huge mistake that was made apparent as

I felt my stomach roll again and the room begin to spin slightly. The hair on the back of my neck stood on end and I knew exactly what the meant. My head snapped in the direction of the only door in the room right before it opened revealing the face of someone, I was hoping I had lost on that ship.

"So, you're awake." He said, placing a wooden tray on the small table beside the bed. I saw a glass of water on it and a stack of small towels. I watched as he walked around to the other side of the bed and sat down in a small black chair. Compared to all the bright colors in the room, it honestly looked out of place. Just like he did.

Kai sat forward and stared me right in the eyes and I sat there unable to look away. I didn't like the way he looked at me. It made me feel like I was completely at his mercy, and I was supposed to be the predator in this situation not him. In this moment however, I felt like anything but.

"Are you feeling better?" He asked. His eyes roamed my body. I knew he was only checking to see if he could see any visible injuries, but it felt like he was doing a little bit more than that. Suddenly the room was feeling a little stuffy and if I could get my body to listen to me and move, I would've attempted another escape. Unfortunately, that wasn't the case.

I didn't want to take my eyes from Kai, I felt like if I did that would be the moment he attacked. Like the moment I looked away, when I turned back, somehow, I would be staring back at my father. It was a crazy thought, but I couldn't help but have it. I didn't want to look away, but I couldn't help but take in more of my surroundings.

Such a strange place, we weren't back on the ship. This wasn't the room I was used to but it also wasn't the room that had kept me prisoner for all those years. The confusion must've been evident on my face because Kai spoke my silent question out loud.

"You're probably wondering where you are." My eyes connected with his and I watched as he sighed and leaned back in his chair. "I guess you wouldn't remember anything after you passed out. This is Milo, my first mate's home. He's letting me borrow it while he helps get the ship ready for departure."

I eyed him suspiciously. "How did you find me?" I asked. The silent treatment wasn't going to get me what I wanted in this situation and what I wanted most right now I realized were answers. Not just where I was and how I got here. I wanted to know how long he had been working with my father and what did he know about Cira?

He smirked. "It wasn't hard, I just looked for a girl passed out on a street corner and just like that, there you were." He was making jokes, but I'm not sure what about my face told him I was in a joking mood. He must've realized that because he sat up straighter and the smile disappeared from his face. "Do you remember passing out on the street?" I hesitated before nodding. I remembered everything about what happened. I remembered the terrible pain in my belly, a pain I was still feeling the remnants of right now. I remember throwing up the blood I had just consumed, and I remembered feeling so lightheaded I couldn't even think straight.

What I didn't remember was how I got from that street corner to this strange bedroom. "I want to know how you tracked me down." It was becoming increasingly difficult to get the words out. The more I talked, the more I began to realize how dry my throat had become.

Kai noticed the crack my voice made at the end of my sentence. He got to his feet making his way to the other side of the table, grabbing the glass of water he'd placed there before and holding it out to me. I stared at it, wondering if he had put something in it. There wasn't much that could poison me and definitely nothing that a human could easily access, but if he really was one of my father's men then he would know the few things that could do me harm. Could I trust him?

There was a moment of silence between us. I stared at the glass, and he stared at me. He sighed and pulled back the glass bringing it to his lips and taking a huge gulp of it. I was so entranced by the bobbing of his Adam's apple and the small droplet of water that slid from his lips down his chin and then cascading down his throat before disappearing underneath his shirt collar. I almost jumped when he shoved the glass back in my face for me to drink. "I'm not trying to poison you, just drink it." I grabbed the glass from him, took one last look at it to make sure there wasn't anything strange floating in it before putting it to my lips and letting the cool liquid slide down my throat.

My shoulders slumped a little in relief. It was ice cold, and I didn't realize how dry my throat was until the moment I had that glass to my lips. I finished the entire thing in seconds. Kai reached out and pulled the glass from my lips, sitting it back on the table and returning to his seat on the other side of the bed.

He sat there quietly staring at me and I stared back at him with a face he would probably describe as confusion. He seemed different from before. Angry maybe? Less patient like I was being an annoyance to him but if anyone was going to be angry it should be me and not him. He was the one that betrayed me. Kai's been working for my father this whole time; he couldn't be trusted.

"I think you owe me an explanation." I owe him? He was definitely one of my father's men just as arrogant as I remember them being. How have I never noticed this about him before?

"You are the one who has explaining to do." Now that I could speak again, I was going to get all the answers I needed from him. I wasn't going to allow him to get anything out of me to take back to my father. "How long have you been working with my father?"

The look on his face quickly changed from irritation to one of pure anger, but I wasn't buying it. He wouldn't fool me again.

"I told you before I have nothing to do with your father." Kai shouted, throwing his hands up in frustration. He scooted his chair closer and placed his elbows on his knees, leaning forward. "You won't use that as an excuse to try to escape again. I want to know who Cira is and I want to know who that is now."

The rage I was beginning to feel when he said her name started in my temples and I could slowly feel my entire body begin to heat up. He was lying and he wasn't even trying to hide it. "If you have no relationship with my father, how do you know that name? No one is supposed to know that name."

"Who is it?" He asked again and with as much strength as I could muster, trying to put the pains in my belly out of my head, I got to my feet and once again had him pinned to the wall. I had the upper hand for only a few seconds, Kai was more prepared this time because before I knew what was happening, I was flat on my back on the bed. My arms were pinned above my head and Kai stared down at me. "That's not going to work this time." He was getting stronger. Was this the effects of the mark or was this just because I hadn't recovered my full strength back yet?

I couldn't contemplate for too long because one second, I was staring into those bright blue eyes and the next I had his soft full lips on mine and any thoughts I had in my head instantly went out the window. I could only think about those lips and how they set my entire body on fire.

My hands were still pinned above my head so the only way I could think of getting him off me was to try to wiggle free. I made a few attempts to slide out from under him, but I quickly realized how bad of an idea it was when I realized I could feel his length rubbing against my inner thigh with every move I made. The heat from that body part was causing little trembles to begin between my legs.

Kai wasn't satisfied with just the little sucking motion he was performing on my bottom lip and if I had to admit it to myself, I wasn't either, so when I felt his warm tongue slide between my lips my entire body melted.

It felt like in this moment, every bone in my body turned to jelly and the only thing my mind could focus on was Kai and his magic ability to make a creature as powerful as me completely at his mercy. The pain in my belly was either completely gone or completely forgotten either way I was more than grateful for at least that much.

Kai let go of my wrists long enough to rub his hands along my sides, leaving a trail of fire in their wake. It felt amazing and in this very moment, I didn't want it to end. Unfortunately, just like everything else in my life, I didn't get what I wanted. Kai's hands disappeared from my skin, leaving me feeling cold and with a small sinking feeling in my stomach that I could only describe as a feeling of rejection.

I took a moment to catch my breath before sitting up on my elbows. Kai returned to his seat, but this time he avoided eye contact with me. Like it pained him to even look my way. "I shouldn't have done that." No, he shouldn't have but now I couldn't help but think I wanted him to do it again.

My mind flashed back to those small moments we had together on the ship. The night I left that mark on his neck. I needed a distraction, so I asked the question that immediately popped into my head. A question that I felt depending on how he answered would crush me. "Did you let me mark you knowing what it meant?" That question made him look up at me and I held my breath while I waited for the answer.

Kai scrubbed his face with his hand before looking back at me. "You know what's funny to me." He said as he got to his feet and began pacing back and forth in front of the bed. "You keep trying to find reason after reason to not trust me when since the moment I meant you, you haven't done one thing to make me put my trust in you." He stopped pacing to face me, placing his hands on his hips. "Yet, for some reason I do. Isn't that strange?"

I wanted to answer, but for some reason I felt like I shouldn't. Like his question was more for himself than for me. "I'm not answering anymore of your questions until you answer mine. I want to know who Cira is and what she has to do with me."

Moving closer to the edge of the bed so my legs dangled over the edge. I took a moment to think about what I would say. Kai was right, I had questioned him at every turn. I stowed away on his ship, marked him which put his life in danger and now I've attacked him not once but twice because I'm just so convinced that he's in cahoots with my father. I don't even have proof that any of that is true. After everything I've done to him, the least I could do was finally answer some questions and maybe he could explain to me where he heard that name.

"I'll tell you what you want to know if..." I got to my feet so I could look him in the eyes. "If you tell me how you know that name."

"I told you already." He threw his hands up in frustration, turning his back to me. "I don't know how, I just heard it."

"What do you mean you heard it? Where? Where did you hear it?" I needed to know, and I couldn't wait a moment longer.

There was a long stretch of time when I didn't get a response from him. The moment seemed so long that for a second, I had to wonder if I even asked the question out loud or not.

"In my head." He finally admitted, turning to face me. "I heard a voice in my head that sounded a lot like you, saying that name."

My heart skipped a beat and suddenly that pain in my belly that I was so sure was gone, had come back tenfold. The panic was setting in quickly. If I were anybody else, I might've laughed at his strange claim, but I was me and, in my world, this wasn't unusual.

I knew the bond behind the mark was strong, but I didn't know it would be the same with a human. When two vampires mark each other things like hearing each other's thoughts was one of the first little tricks you acquired, but since Kai was human and he couldn't mark me, I figured that was something we wouldn't have to deal with.

With the more time we spent together, our bond was getting stronger, not weaker like I was hoping it was. If Kai was developing the ability to hear my thoughts, how was I going to be able to disappear from him without him finding me.

My mind was racing a mile a minute, and I guess that was beginning to show on my face because the next thing that came out of his mouth was a question, I was hoping he wouldn't ask. "You knew this was going happen, didn't you?" I couldn't lie the accusation stung a little. This was just as new to me as it was to him, but I guess I couldn't blame him for not knowing that even though marks were common where I'm from, they weren't common with humans. "What else have you been keeping from me?"

I looked away from him, instead focusing on a spot in the carpeting on the floor. "Answer me, Niyla. Is that even your real name."

"Fine." I threw my hands up in the air in frustration. This wasn't getting us anywhere. He was hiding things from me, and I was hiding things from him. "Marked mates do display a few *extra* abilities that those that aren't mated don't."

"What the hell does that mean?" He asked clear frustration in his voice. "What else is supposed to happen to me? You told me I wouldn't become-"

"You won't." I cut him off, trying to provide at least a little reassurance. "You won't become one, you'll just have a few enhanced abilities." In other words, he'll have all the benefits of being one of us without all the downsides.

I sighed. "Look, our *situation* is unique. There aren't any humans who have been marked by a vampire where I'm from. I've heard rumors that they existed in the past, but I've never actually been able to confirm. I'm learning just like you are."

"So, you're saying you have no idea how much I'm going to change?" The way he looked at me was almost like he was pleading with me to have all the answers, but as much as I hated to admit it, I didn't. Instead, I decided to change the subject.

"I answered your question, now you answer mine." I folded my arms across my chest and sat back on the edge of the bed. I didn't like the disappointed look on his face at hearing that

I couldn't give him more information and I was feeling this strong urge to wrap my arms around him. "Do you have anything to do with that guard showing up at the port?"

"I told you before, I don't and I'm not lying. At some point you're going to have to learn to trust someone. Now it's your turn, who is Cira?"

I bit the inside of my cheek. I could taste the blood trickling into my mouth but instead of the metallic taste I was used to, all I tasted was dirt. This was a topic of conversation I haven't even been able to have with my own family and now I was about to have it with essentially a stranger.

"Cira was my sister. She died a long time ago." I couldn't bear to look at him while I spoke, so I dropped my eyes back to the floor. "The last time I saw my sister was when she was leaving my bedroom after giving me my last bedtime story over a hundred and forty years ago."

"Over a hundred and forty years!" The shock was expected, after all we are called *immortals* for a reason. "I guess the myths about Vampires are true, but I don't understand. When I heard you thinking about her, you said that you didn't want me to end up like her. Why would I end up like someone who died so long ago?"

A shiver ran down my back when I thought about what I had learned and I really didn't want to tell him, but I said I would tell him the truth and that's exactly what I was going to do. "I learned a few years later, that my sister didn't just disappear like I was told. There was talk that she was taken because my father found out about the mistake she had made."

"What mistake?"

"Cira, she had marked a human." I could feel the tears welling up in my eyes when I thought about what was going to happen to Kai if my father ever found out. I raised my head to meet his eyes before I spoke again. "You see now don't you, because I marked you the same will happen to me and you."

Chapter 11

Since I've meant this mysterious vampire girl almost a week ago, I thought for sure by now I had heard everything. From the mark she put on me, to the enhanced strength and now even the mind reading. All of this had been something straight out of a Syfy movie, but even this wasn't something I was expecting.

Because of what she did to me, now I was going to be hunted down and killed? What the hell was I supposed to do with that piece of information? My leg began to twitch, and it took everything in me to stay in my seat.

"So, you're saying, your sister put a mark on some human guy like you did to me and because of that your own family killed both of them?" Niyla nodded slowly. I was expecting an instant feeling of dread for my impending death to overcome me, but instead I felt more panicked over her being killed because of me than me being killed.

I don't care who was coming after her. Human or vampire, there was no way I was letting them come anywhere near her.

"If you knew that this would be the outcome, what was your plan, ditch me and then what? Try to take them on yourself?"

"I didn't have a plan ok." She huffed. I was trying my hardest not to feel bad for her, after all this situation was all her doing. If she hadn't run away from home and stowed away on my ship. If she hadn't bitten me and left this mark behind, all of this was because of the choices she made, but I couldn't help but think about the things that led her to making these decisions. Her father going as far as killing one daughter because she stepped out of line and imprisoning the other to prevent her from doing the same thing. She's been locked up for who knows how long and the first chance she got to be free, she took it. Could I really blame her for that? I know if I was in her situation, I might've done the same.

"After my sister disappeared, I was left alone in that place to deal with my father and all his rules by myself. I had to dress the way he wanted me to, say what he wanted me to and when he offered me a year of freedom to do what I wanted, he just had to add a small stipulation. When I return home after my year, I was to marry who he had chosen for me."

An arranged marriage. That was her breaking point. I guess it made sense she had been controlled by her father all her life and now she would be controlled by someone in her father's control. Anyone would run away from a situation like that. Her actions all made sense now, but there was one thing she said that stood out to me. Something that didn't make complete sense.

"I thought you said your sister died." It was a statement but one I wanted her to answer. She looked at me in confusion, so I elaborated. "Just now you said she disappeared. Did she die, or did she disappear?"

The confused look on her face didn't change. "I told you what I was told, that she died because she marked a human. *Disappeared*, or *died* what's the difference? My sister is gone that's all that matters."

I sat forward in my chair and reached out so I could grab her hands. "There is a difference." I wonder why she had never thought of this fact. I guess that's what happens when you're forced to believe everything someone tells you your entire life, you learn not to question things that you should. "Are you sure your sister was actually killed?" Her face changed into one of realization then she gave me a smile that didn't quite reach her eyes and a little scoff.

"That's a nice thought, but I know how long it's been since I've seen my sister. What do you think happened, they locked her in some secret part of the castle, and she's been there this whole time?"

Yes, it was a crazy idea, but everything about this situation is crazy. Vampires, arranged marriages, but suddenly faking deaths was just out of the realm of possibility. "Were there any witnesses to her death or better yet, does she even have a gravesite."

She hesitated, biting her lip a little before answering. "Of course not, my family wont even allow people to speak her name. They practically erased her from existence, no pictures, nothing. You think they would allow a gravesite." She emphasized her point with a little eyeroll.

I squeezed her hands a little tighter. "Think about it this way, would you rather be the daughter of people who would kill their own daughter or be the daughter of people who would *lie* about killing their own daughter?" There was that hesitation again, like she wanted to believe me, but it went against everything she had ever believed about the people who had raised her. "You have to at least consider the idea that there may be a chance, she could be alive."

It took a minute, but finally I caught the small movement of her nodding her head. Something like this for anyone would be hard to believe. If what she says is true, then for over a hundred years she had been believing that her sister was dead all because she made the mistake of marking a human.

Niyla pulled her hands from mine, sitting back on the bed and rubbing her hands on her jeans nervously. "If this is all true, what am I supposed to do now? I have no way of proving if Cira is still alive or where she would be if she was."

"Have you ever thought about what happened to the human she marked?"

She shook her head no. "I just assumed he was killed when she was, but now I don't know what to believe." Niyla lifted her hand up and began running it through her hair disrupting the already messy lose curls. The panic was beginning to show on her face. I needed to do something before she started spiraling; this was clearly something she wasn't expecting to ever have to think about again. Now that she has to face this possibility, it was obvious she was starting to freak out.

I would help her find out the truth however I could, and with any luck it'll help us figure out a way to not end up anymore on the wrong end of her father's wrath than we already were. Right now though, I wanted to take her mind off it, even if it was just for a little while and the only way I could think of doing was to feed the urge I'd had the moment she woke up and I saw those strange grey eyes of hers.

In one swift movement, I slid from my chair across to the bed, sitting so close that my thigh rubbed up against hers. Since she disappeared from the ship two days ago, it has felt like my skin was crawling and no matter how I tried to distract myself, nothing seemed to make it stop. Now, even with this small amount of contact through our clothes, I could already feel myself beginning to calm down. The effects of the mark were so strange, and now it was making me wonder, if we are supposed to separate after all of this, would I have to feel like that forever? She said eventually the longer we're apart, the more the bond would fade. Could I believe her, was I even willing to take that risk? Right now, the thought of us being apart for even a little while longer, made me want to tear my hair out from the roots.

Niyla didn't meet my eyes, instead she kept her focus on her sock cladded feet. It made my heart skip a beat that I could still make her nervous after all we had done together. She had lived so many years but had so little life experience. I wanted to change that. I wanted to take her aboard my ship and travel the world with her, showing her everything she had been missing out on.

I slipped my hand underneath hers, threading my fingers through hers. Her hand felt warm and a little sweaty. Why did I find it a little funny that she could get sweaty palms. If I didn't know any better, I would say she was a normal young girl and not a hundred-year-old being who drank blood and could overpower me whenever she felt like it.

"You know you don't have to be nervous around me, right?" She nodded her head but still didn't look up. Shelving my hand under her chin I turned her head so I could see those eyes.

Those eyes, this greyish color would be my new favorite color along with the rosy color of her lips. Lips that I was starting to realize would be my new obsession. So plump and soft and all mines.

I leaned close and waited to see if she would pull away from me, when she didn't, I closed the gap between our lips and felt a shock to my nervous system when my lips touched hers. My entire body relaxed, and I leaned into her more, applying more pressure to her lips. She tasted so sweet, and I felt completely consumed by such a small kiss. It was like I had gone days without water, and she was like a tall, ice-cold glass of exactly what I needed.

Her hand slipped from mine, and she wrapped them both around my neck pulling me closer. I wanted her and it was clear the feeling was mutual. If her sister was dead or alive, if her father had killed her human mate and was now going to do the same to me. All of that didn't matter now, that would be tomorrow's problem. For now, all I could think about was how long it would take to strip her of her clothes and get her underneath me. I wanted to have her panting and begging me for release and then I wanted to give it to her repeatedly.

Niyla pulled away and began working on the buttons of my shirt, but I stopped her before she could get very far. Last time and even the time before that, she took care of me, this time I would be taking care of her. She must've misunderstood my actions as rejection because she began to pull away, but before she could completely close herself off, I pushed on her shoulders making her lay back on the bed and climbed on top of her.

She stared into my eyes as I leaned in to give her a small peck on the side of her neck. Grabbing the bottom of her black T-shirt, in one swift motion I slid it up and over her head. My eyes drifted down to her bare chest, no bra to impede my sight and there was much better lighting here than in my quarters on my ship. I could see everything, and I enjoyed every last little bit of it.

Her breasts were perky, and just a little more than a handful for me. Considering how large my hands were, the sight was enough to make my cock jump. I wonder what it would feel like to slide my aching cock between the valley of her breasts, probably just like sliding into heaven.

Those brown perfect nipples, ripe and ready for me. I leaned in and drew one of them between my lips, sucking slightly. Niyla shifted beneath me, letting out a soft moan.

I couldn't help the smirk that played on my lips as I pulled back, looking up at her face. "You like that baby?" I didn't need her to answer but when she gave me a breathy *yes*, I felt another enormous amount of blood rush straight to my cock.

Shit was there anything this girl could do to turn me off. Just with that one word I felt like I could bust an entire load in my pants right now.

I got back to work on those sexy nipples, stroking them gently with my togue and giving little teasing nips with my teeth. She squirmed more, pressing her pelvis into my aching cock. It only succeeded in making the space in my pants even tighter.

I was really trying to keep my self-control intact so I could make this as good for her as possible, but she was making that extremely difficult. While my mouth focused on her delicious nipples, my hand got to work on the buttons of her jeans. I impressed myself with how fast I managed to pop open the button and slide the rough material past her hips.

I pulled away long enough to pull the jeans the rest of the way down, tossing them to the side.

Before I could get my hands on those panties so I could see what was underneath, her hands shot out to cover herself. If I wasn't so turned on right now, I would probably see this as another display of her cute and innocent shyness, but at this very moment, all I could wrap my mind around was getting her legs wrapped around my head as quickly as possible. The shyness was going to have to be saved for another time.

I grabbed both of her wrists and held them above her head with one hand. She struggled to break free and even with this new enhanced strength I had, I had this slight suspicion that she didn't put that much effort into trying to break free.

So, she liked a little restraint, I made a mental note of that for later. She looked up at me, waiting to see what my next move was, so I leaned in and pressed my lips against hers and I felt her body relax. While I distracted her with my lips, my hand slipped past the waist band of her panties. It didn't take any time at all for me to feel the moist folds between her legs. I couldn't help but moan at how slick she felt. She was so wet for me. I knew I wasn't the only one having an extremely strong reaction to being close again. Her mouth could deny it but there was no way her body could.

Her hips lifted off the bed, almost like she was trying to guide my hand right where she wanted it, so that's exactly what I let her do. I slipped my tongue past her lips just as she shifted her hips at just the right angle for my finger to slip past the tight ring of her opening. She let out a surprised squeak and I instantly stopped moving. I never really thought about it before, but I guess given her previous living situation it was something that should've crossed my mind.

I pulled back so I could look her in the eyes. I watched as she pulled her bottom lip between her teeth and began to chew on it. Her eyes darted around trying to avoid mine. I bet she knew what I was going to say.

"This is your first time."

"No." Her response was almost immediate and clearly a lie, but I wouldn't press the matter. Nothing changed, except now I needed to make sure my actions were a lot slower and much gentler. This would be a true test of my self-control, but for her it was becoming increasingly apparent that I would do anything for her.

No more talking was needed. I leaned in and gave her a quick kiss on the lips before sliding down her body. I didn't stop until I came face to face with the white lace that covered the area I so desperately wanted to taste.

Gripping both sides of the lace, I pulled them off, tossing them over my shoulder to join her jeans. I grabbed both of her thighs and lifted them up spreading her wide so I could see everything.

Those pink folds dripping with arousal and not one speck of hair in sight. I wondered if that was her doing, or was she just naturally smooth. I didn't have time to contemplate it for too long, I wanted my mouth on her so without any hesitation, I stuck out my tongue and leaned in for my first taste. Her taste was like a burst on my tongue, just like I imagined it would be. I was so lightheaded, I was starting to see stars. That's what she did to me.

Her hips jolted and she tried to pull away from me, but I wasn't letting that happen. I tightened my grip on her thighs and pulled her closer to me, leaning in so I could devour her.

With my face buried deep in between her thighs, I got to work licking up all the juices that flowed out of her like a never-ending river. God, she tasted amazing. I don't think I could ever get enough of it. I pressed my face in tighter, kissing those sweet lips gently before moving up to play with her clit with my tongue.

Niyla moaned and shifted her hips, first attempting to move away from my continuous attack on her sensitive area and then grounding her hips against my face, begging for more. If she wanted more that's exactly what I would give her. Releasing one of her thighs, I placed one finger at her entrance and began messaging it slightly until it gave way to the very tip of my finger. Her breathing hitched but she gave up trying to get away, instead she spread her legs wider for me.

Pressing my finger in further, I doubled the efforts of my tongue on her clit. It took only a second for the moans coming from her to grow louder. Her back began to arch off the bed and her legs began to shake. The juices coming from her began to flow more rapidly and I licked even faster until she gave one loud scream, and her muscles began to contract around my finger. I pumped my finger in and out of her until the seizing of her body began to subside and her muscles finally relaxed.

Pulling my finger out, I kissed my way up her body. First her inner thigh, belly, the valley between her breasts, then her neck until I was able to look at her face. She had her eyes closed but the look on her face was pure ecstasy and I couldn't help but feel the pride swell in my chest at the knowledge that I had given that to her.

"How was it baby?" I asked. Another stroke to my ego wouldn't hurt anyone.

Chapter 12

The way he touched me, kissed me, how he knew how to handle my body like this was something he had been doing for years. Everything about what was happening now was perfect. Those secret moments I shared with a few of the servants back home were nothing compared to any moment I've spent with Kai. I don't think after how sweet and understanding he has been about the things he's learned about me, that I could still say what was happening between us was only because of the mark. I couldn't keep denying my attraction to him both physically and emotionally. I was falling for him, and I didn't know how to handle it.

Kai didn't wait for me to answer, instead, he climbed off the bed and striped from head to toe leaving himself completely bare to my eyes. I could feel my cheeks heating up and I wanted to look away, but I couldn't bring myself to do it. He was not made the same way as those other men. He was all hard-earned muscle. Years of being aboard a ship loading and unloading various boxes and heavy crates made him like this.

My eyes roamed over his entire body until they finally landed on his face, that's when I noticed he was smiling at me. The way his eyes looked at me, I saw such strange emotions in them, ones I wasn't sure I could describe. It almost looked like he was admiring me, and I had to wonder if the way I looked at him matched the way he looked at me.

"You're so beautiful." He climbed back onto the bed, crawling up my body so he was face to face with me and his lower half lined up perfectly with mine. Kai's body felt a little heavy on top of mine, but strangely instead of feeling crushed, I welcomed the weight. He leaned in and gave me a peck on my lips, then my cheek and neck.

"Are you ready for me baby?" I hesitated, contemplating if this was the right thing to do with everything else that was going on. My father was after the both of us, before everything was all over, we could both end up dead just like my sister and her mate. I was supposed to be distancing myself from him so that it would be easier for him to move on with his life. Was this really the best thing to do? I could live with it hurting me in the end, but I don't think I would be able to survive hurting him.

I felt his hand rub my thigh gently and I brought my eyes back up to his. "Where did you go?" He asked. I shook my head. I didn't want to tell him. This was supposed to be a sweet moment between us where we could phase out the rest of the world and just focus on each other. I didn't want to ruin that by bringing reality back in. "I think we've proven by now that you can tell me anything."

He was right, but I couldn't talk to him about this, so instead of telling him the truth, I settled to give him my best smile and giving him the simplest answer I could. "I was just thinking about you."

He eyed me almost like he didn't believe me, but I guess he decided now wasn't the best time to press the topic. "That's good, I'm thinking about you too." Kai shifted his position, so he kneeled on the bed and pulled me on top of him. He positioned me so I wrapped my legs around his waist with my center hovering just above his member and his hands held firmly to my hips. I wrapped my arms around his neck to help keep myself balanced.

"Relax," He cooed. "I got you." He pressed down on my hips slightly and I followed his lead, lowering myself until I felt the tip of him pressing at my entrance. My heart skipped a beat, but I tried to force myself to relax. I could do this. I wanted to do this. I wanted to be with Kai this way and I knew he wouldn't hurt me, so I had no idea why I was so nervous.

There was a pause, where Kai stopped pressing and just stared into my eyes, I guess he was giving me a chance to change my mind and that alone made me want to be with him even more. I tightened my grip around his neck, pulling him closer to me and placing my head in the crock of his neck. Angling my hips slightly, I pushed down until I felt the sting of his member slide inside of me.

My back stiffened and I stilled instantly. Oh god, why did it hurt so much. I instantly began questioning if I would be able to go through with this after all.

Kai shushed me and rubbed my back gently trying to soothe me. When I relaxed a little in his arms, he took that as the opportunity to tighten his grip on me, raise his hips causing me to slide further down on him and knocking the wind out of me. The small shriek that came out of me was involuntary as well as the way I tightened my thighs around him.

"It's ok baby, I got you. Whenever you're ready."

I shifted my hips back and forth trying to help ease some of the sting. It took a little while and Kai waited patiently.

Kai groaned when I pulled back from him and began kissing on the side of his neck. "God, you're making it so hard to be a gentleman right now."

I couldn't help but smile. Being born immortal means I spent my entire life feeling like I was stronger and much more power-ful than millions of others, but I don't think I've ever felt more powerful than I do at this very moment.

The grinding of my hips gradually changed into more of a bounce on Kai's lap. The more I moved, the better it felt. Kai groaned and squeezed me tighter. If the sounds he was making was any indicator, he was feeling just as good as I was and I was gradually beginning to feel amazing.

With every twist and turn I made on top of him, I felt little bolts of lightning shooting through every nerve ending in my body. God, this felt amazing. I moved faster against him, and it wasn't long before he began matching my movements. Whenever I slid down on him, he would raise his hips to meet mine. A pressure began to build in my lower belly, and I started to feel little flutters at my core. Faster, I moved, my heart desperately working to pump more air into my lungs.

In that moment, it was like my body had a mind of its own. My fangs descended and the only thing I could think about was taking Kai's blood. I didn't care to ask if he wanted me to, I didn't think about what it would do to the bond we were both already feeling the strong effects of. None of that mattered at this moment, all that mattered was the warm, sweet blood rushing through his veins and how I desperately wanted to take it.

Leaning in, I opened my mouth wide and sunk my fangs into the side of his neck. He flinched, clearly not expecting my bite. With the first tug on his veins, his moans grew louder. His upward thrusts grew more urgent.

His blood tasted just as amazing as I remember. It was almost drugging, it made me feel like I was floating on a cloud. The euphoria from his blood mixed with the addicting pressure I was feeling grow between my legs had me completely delirious. If we survived my family, and Kai wanted to be with me, is this how it would always be? Would this private time we spent together be this earth shattering? My mouth filled with his blood, and I greedily gulped it down tightening my thighs around his waist as the pressure built even more.

Kai groaned. "Come for me baby. I want to come together." I wanted that too and with one final upward pump from Kai that's exactly what happened. All the air rushed from my lungs and stars danced behind my eyes.

My body seized up and for a second, I felt like I was floating. The only thing that brought me back to Earth was the oddly sexy sounds that Kai made as he reached his peek. His hips jerked in quick concession as he moaned out my name, and I could feel the muscles in his abs tighten as he crushed his body against mine.

I pulled my fangs from his neck, licking the incisions free of any extra blood to help them close. It didn't take long before his hips slowed their bucking, and his body relaxed against mine.

He gave me a gentle kiss on my cheek, rubbing my back slowly. I basked in the feelings that welled up while I was being soothed by him.

It seemed like we laid there forever, but when the first draft hit my sweat soaked, heated skin, I came back to my senses. I slipped from his grip and untangled my limbs from him. Sliding across the bed, I grabbed the blankets to wrap around my naked body. I don't know why I would be nervous; he had already seen everything. Maybe I was embarrassed with how drunk I got from his blood. No, not just his blood, his body too.

Kai smiled at me and reached out his hand to rub my bare thigh. His touch was like an electric shock to my nervous system. How strange, we just had sex, but I could feel the quivering between my legs returning. I wanted him inside me again. To feel connected with him again. "It's a little late to be embarrassed, don't you agree?"

I opened my mouth to try and dispute his comment. To tell him it doesn't matter what we just did, if I wanted to be embarrassed to have him look at my naked body then I had a right to do just that. I didn't have a chance to say anything because my ears suddenly picked up a strange noise coming from outside of the room.

It was such a faint sound that for a spit second, I thought I had imagined it. That is until I heard it again. Almost like a scuffle, like something was scraping against hardwood floors.

"What's that look on your face?" Kai asked me. I don't know how my face must've looked to him, but I imagined the way

I had it all scrunched up was probably very alarming to him considering what we had just done.

"Are we alone here?" I asked, never taking my eyes off the door. The noise wasn't getting louder, but it was getting closer and as what happens naturally to any vampire when we feel an impending threat, all the muscles in my body began to tighten, preparing for an attack.

"What do you mean?" I guess the enhanced hearing wasn't something he had developed with the bond, or at least it hadn't kicked in yet.

I didn't respond to his question, instead I scrambled off the bed, scooping my clothes from the floor and putting them on as quickly as I could. Kai didn't question me anymore, he hopped up and began pulling his clothes on as well, a lot slower than I was but at least he wouldn't be completely nude when whoever else was lurking around this place decided to attack.

With every article of clothing I slipped on, I never took my eyes off the door. The strange noise got closer until it was right outside the door. I stood up straight and stared at the door, holding my breath, and trying to prepare for what was going to happen next. Was it my father's men, had they found us and were now going to take me back to the castle and kill Kai or was it another option that I would find very hard to believe right now which was a simple burglar trying to see what they could covet. From the corner of my eye, I saw Kai slipping his last boot on and standing up, staring at me in confusion. There wasn't time to explain and, in a few minutes, if I was right and there was someone else in the house, I wouldn't need to.

"What's wrong?" He asked.

I held my finger to my lips, telling him to stay quiet just as I seen the brass doorknob slowly beginning to turn. I spread my legs apart and squared my shoulders, getting into a fighting stance. Over the years, my father had made it mandatory for me to learn every fighting style available. I always thought it was stupid because who would I ever need to fight, but at this very moment I was thankful for it.

Just as the door creaked on its hinges, the window behind me shattered. I ducked covering my head from the flying glass shards. I looked to my right, peering through the small gap between the underside of the bed and the floor, and I could see Kai laying facedown with his hands covering his head.

I tried to turn to see what had broken the window when I felt a few shards of glass cut my cheek. I closed my eyes to prevent any flying glass from getting in them. I couldn't see and whoever entered the room took that as an opportunity to attack.

I heard Kai shout out in pain. I turned my head and opened my eyes to look under the bed again, but there was suddenly smoke filling the room and I could barely see in front of me, let alone on the other side of this giant piece of furniture.

"Kai!" I called out for him, but all I got in return were what sounded like pain induced grunts. I tried getting to my feet. The smoke filled the room quickly and very soon it was a thick cloud of gray, and I could barely see my hands in front of me.

Someone grabbed my arm, snatching me up and pressing me close to their chest. I instantly knew it wasn't Kai. Instead of feeling safe and comforted and an undeniable sense of trust, the way I usually did when I was in his arms, I felt rolling waves of disgust. I didn't know who this person was, but he wasn't my mate.

The stranger leaned in by my ear and whispered something that sent an instant chill down my spine. "Hey baby, did you miss me."

Chapter 13

An ice-cold shiver went down my spine. A voice I hadn't heard since I left home. Not the voice I was expecting to hear but one that I was hoping to never hear again. I could feel the bile begin to rise in my throat and it took everything I had not to throw up right there at the mere thought that he had his hands on my body. Shifting, I tried to loosen his grip, but that only made him tighten it even more.

"What's wrong sweetness? I thought you would've missed your husband to be."

Another wave of nausea. I shifted in his arms some more, just enough so that I could turn to face him and even with the smoke screen filling the room, I could see those bright blonde curls framing a face that stared at me with a smug expression. All that facial hair, that made him look just like the beast that he was proving to be. Laurel.

"Laurel, get your hands off of me." I said through clenched teeth. Squirming more, I tried my hardest to get his hands off, but I couldn't understand why he was so much stronger than me. Only pure-blooded vampires could be this strong and I knew all the pure-blooded families, he wasn't part of one.

"Aww sweetness, you should learn to be a lot more affection-ate with the man you're going to marry. You know, I'm really hurt that you tried to run away from me, I thought we really had something special." He leaned in and for a second, it looked like he was going to kiss me, so I craned my neck trying to avoid his lips.

"What do you want us to do with him?" There was a voice behind me causing him to freeze and look up at whoever was talking. I used his distraction as a chance to break free of his grip. Spinning around, I watched in horror as the guard we'd seen at the pier held Kai by the throat.

Kai clawed at his hands, struggling to breathe. His lips begin-ning to turn a slight shade of blue. I took a step towards them when Laurel grabbed my arm, pulling me back.

"Not so fast sweetness. We weren't done catching up yet and what better way to do that then over a nice meal." He stretched out his arm in the direction of Kai and the guard in a dramatic flair. "Look at that, you even provided the dinner. You really are too sweet for your own good." Laurel pulled me close and before I could stop him, he planted a kiss right on my lips, just for Kai to see.

He licked the seam of my lips trying to get me to open my mouth, but I kept my lips pressed tightly together. I feared the moment I opened my mouth is the moment the vomit I had been holding in would finally make an appearance and as much as that would be so satisfying to do to him, now was not the time.

He pressed his lips harder against mine, but finally pulled back when he realized I wasn't going to give in. "So, love," he said releasing me. "Do you want the first bite or shall I?" Laurel pushed me to the side approaching Kai and the guard.

When he got close enough, the guard released Kai and he crumbled to the floor, struggling to catch his breath. I watched Laurel crouched down, so he was eye level with Kai. I wanted to rush to his side, to protect him from Laurel even touching him, but I was worried that he would snap his neck before I could even take a step.

My hands began to sweat as I was forced to watch Laurel make a full assessment of Kai. His eyes roaming over every part of his body. All I could think was had he seen the mark yet and when he does what would he do? Would he kill him on the spot and then follow it up with ending my life? Would he contact my father and take us back to the castle so that he would have the privilege of killing his last living daughter and the human mate she made the mistake of marking.

"Did you have fun playing with my fiancé, little human?" The way he teased Kai, I could see the vein on his forehead from here, I just hope he wasn't foolish enough to provoke Laurel. He had to understand after all this that he was much stronger than Kai and that it wouldn't be smart to try to pick a fight with him.

Kai took a few more gasps of air before trying to speak. "You touch her again… I'll rip your face off."

My heart skipped a beat. I really wish he hadn't said that. While it was incredibly sexy, I also knew how someone like Laurel would take a comment like that especially coming from a human. Just like I thought, he lifted his fist up high and before I had a chance to react, he brought it down hitting Kai in the jaw so hard his head whipped to the side, blood flying from his mouth as he collapsed. I covered my mouth trying to hold in my scream as I felt a splitting headache begin radiating through my head. If I screamed out, Laurel would be able to figure out that Kai and I were connected. Until I figured out a plan, I couldn't let that happen.

I didn't know what would happen if I stepped in, but I couldn't allow him to continue beating on Kai. Thanks to the mark, any harm that came to him, I could feel too. Pushing past Laurel, I bent down and scooped Kai's unconscious body into my arms, holding his head close to my body. I kept my back to Laurel while I checked over his injuries. His breathing was steady, but already half of his face was starting to swell.

I could hear Laurel snickering behind me. "Don't tell me you actually care for this human." I didn't justify his claim with a response, instead I tried focusing on Kai and trying to figure out how I was going to get us out of this situation safely.

"I am talking to you. You have no right to ignore me, especially not for some blood bag." Laurel grabbed my chin and turned me, so I had no choice but to look at him. I watched as his eyes grew wide in shock and his eyes darted back and forth between Kai and me.

He released my chin and backed away from me. "You slut." I pulled Kai closer to me. He knew. Laurel knew what I had done and now I wasn't sure what he would do. "You marked that filthy human didn't you." I chewed on my lip and looked away from him and that's when I caught a glimpse of myself in the reflection of the shiny wood of the bedframe. Half of my face had begun to swell the same way Kai's had. This is what Laurel saw. Kai's injuries were reflecting on my body. There was no way to hide the mark anymore, no way to deny it. Laurel would tell my father; Kai would die, and it would be all my fault.

Laurel stood up and paced back and forth. "Sir, what do you want to do?" The guard asked. He stopped his pacing and stared at the floor. For a long moment he didn't say a word and

I held my breath, hoping for just the smallest amount of mercy. If he would just let us go, we would disappear. Both he and my father would never hear from us again. If that was too much to ask, he could just give us a head start. My father could tell the rest of our people whatever lie he chose. He could tell them I died, hell he had the ability to convince everyone I never existed in the first place.

All we needed was just the smallest flicker of compassion. Laurel finally turned to face us. My stomach dropping when I saw the look on his face. His eyes looked almost wild, and he bared his teeth. I wasn't sure what to make of his expression. Was he angry or deranged, either way, it was very clear that glimmer of compassion I was hoping he would have didn't exist.

"Take them, take them both." There it was, he was going to do exactly what I expected. Take me to my father, tell him I had done exactly what Cira had done and both of us would die. "Let's see what your father has to say about your adulterous little affair with this pathetic human."

The guard grabbed my arm snatching me away from Kai. I struggled against him as I watched Kai's limp body slink back to the floor. I pushed against the guard, but he wouldn't budge. Just like Laurel, for some odd reason he appeared to be stronger than me. What was it about these two, how could they both manage to overpower a pure blood of the Grey family, that was just unheard of.

The guard dragged me away and I had to watch as Laurel stood over Kai's unconscious body still staring at me with that sick look on his face. I screamed out Kai's name hoping he would wake up and try to escape, but even with how loudly I screamed, he didn't move an inch, and I was left helpless to protect him.

I struggled against the guard, trying to get back to him but he just wouldn't budge. I tried my hardest to break free, I barely noticed when the guard grabbed me by each side of my head. He leaned in and whispered, "This is what happens when you lay with a filthy human," and gave my head a sharp twist. A sickening crack was the last thing I heard before everything went black.

I don't know how long I had been out, but when I awoke, I laid flat on my stomach on a damp, cold concrete floor. When I tried to roll onto my back, the pain radiated throughout my entire body, and I let out a groan. It took everything in me to get my eyes open. All I wanted to do was curl up into a ball for warmth and go back to sleep.

"Niyla." I heard someone whisper my name but all I could do was groan in response. "Niyla." I heard the voice again. "You have to wake up, they'll be back soon." Rolling to my side, I opened my eyes and looked in the direction of the voice. There in a far corner, just barely capturing any moonlight I saw the faint glow of Kai's blonde locks.

The memories came flooding back. Laurel had found us in a home that Kai was sure would be safe. He had beaten Kai and found out about the mark. We got separated and now I had no idea where we were. I opened my mouth to speak but no sound came out. My throat was dry and scratchy. I was thirsty. I needed blood. Kai's blood.

I tried pulling myself up to a crawl, but it was as if I had no energy to do it. I felt so weak, kind of how I felt after drinking that drunkard's blood the other night. What was wrong with me? The last person whose blood I drank was Kai's so I should be feeling my strongest now, right?

I heard the rattling of chains before I heard Kai's voice again. "Don't move too much," he said. "They drained you after bringing us here." Drained me? I held up my wrist to examine it and that's when I saw the giant, ugly wound glaring back at me. Even in this terrible lighting, I could see the caked up dried blood covering my entire arm. How much blood did they take from me? They must've used silver to do it. Wounds made by silver take longer to heal especially without being able to feed to help along the process. If they were going to go through all this trouble, why not just kill me then. I was already unconscious, wouldn't that have just been the easier way to go about it?

Dropping my arm, I opened my mouth and tried again to call for Kai. It came out as only a whisper but thankfully he heard me, nonetheless. I heard scuffling coming from him followed by the same loud clanking of chains.

"I can't come any closer, I'm chained." His voice sounded desperate. I heard him make a few grunting noises followed by more rattling chains. There was no way even with his new enhanced strength he would be able to break free from the chains. The only way this would work is if I somehow found the strength to make my way across the room to him and I just didn't have it in me.

"I can't move." I whispered back. It felt like swallowing glass every time I tried to speak.

"It wouldn't matter if you could." A deep baritone voice came from behind me. I silently prayed to myself that it wasn't who I thought it was but considering how my luck had turned out so far, I knew I absolutely would not be so lucky. I lifted just enough to turn my head toward the direction of the voice and sure enough, there on the other side of the prison bars I hadn't noticed before, stood Ezra Grey, my father. He stared at Kai and said, "If she goes anywhere near your blood, I'll remove her head from her shoulders, right here and now."

His eyes turned to look at me, disgust clear on his face. "Welcome back daughter."

Chapter 14

He stood there, glaring at both of us in all his intimidating glory acting as if he was better than us. Then again, I guess that's what he's always told me, *you must always make those beneath you know their position. You must never let them believe they are more than what they are, especially humans. They are nothing more than how we sustain our lives, nothing more, nothing less.* That is how the great Ezra Grey has taught me to treat those that do not share the same power as me, I never thought he would treat his own children the same. I was wrong about a lot of things and if I ever had any doubt before about if he could have the heart to kill his own child, that was all gone now.

A loud creak came from the old metal door as he slid it to the side and stepped inside our prison. He never took his eyes off me as he walked towards me and crouched down to my level. I scrambled trying to put myself in a sitting position so I wouldn't appear as weak as I felt, but all I could manage was an awkward half sit, half lean.

The curls on top of my head were probably an unkept mess. Ezra eyed me before reaching out and brushing one of the chocolate brown curls from my face, brushing it behind my ear. "My darling daughter, look what has become of you."

I jerked my face out of his hold. I hated it when he acted this way. In front of others, Ezra was known for portraying the loving and devoted husband and father, but behind closed doors, he was a monster. A dictator. He was ruthless and merciless and the type of man who would kill his own daughter because she stepped out of line and now because of what I had done, he would do it again.

"Cut the act *Father*, just tell me what you plan to do to us." I wasn't the same girl who'd left this house only a short time ago. I wouldn't allow him to keep this act going so it seemed as if I was the ungrateful daughter who defied her father just because she was going through her rebellious phase. I left that night because I wanted to be free of him and this life and it was very clear that he wasn't going to allow anything other than his way. I don't regret my decision to leave, I don't regret stowing away on Kai's ship and I don't regret meeting him. What I regret is putting him on Ezra's radar. Now whatever happens to him will be all my fault and I wasn't sure I could live with that. I had to get him out of this no matter what, even if it meant I would have to sacrifice myself to do it.

"You've always been such an impatient child, have I ever told you that?" I didn't respond to his question, and I wouldn't say another word to him until he got to the point. I wanted to know what his plan for us was and I wanted to know it now. This wasn't a time for his sick games, this was life or death.

"Fine, I guess it's a crime for a father to show his daughter any affection after she returns from a life changing trip." Ezra got to his feet and made his way across the cell approaching Kai.

"Stay away from him!" I shouted at him. "Your issues are with me; he has nothing to do with this."

"I beg to differ my darling daughter. Everything that happens from now on will be entirely his doing." I looked at Kai and even though in the dim lighting I couldn't see his eyes, I knew he could see mine. It hurt to have him look at me when I knew, everything that was happening was my fault. It was happening to him because of the decisions I made, and it would be my father that would be his death.

I dropped my head in shame. I felt like at this moment I would welcome death with open arms just to stop myself from feeling this way.

"No," I croaked out. "This is my fault, Father. I am the one who marked him, not the other way around, so do not make it seem as though he made me do such a thing. It was my choice and my choice alone." I brought my eyes back up to first look at Ezra who turned to face me then back to Kai as I said, "I am the one who tricked him into this. He was my victim."

The cell was eerily quiet. Nobody spoke and it even seemed as though all the sounds of nature that could be heard through the small opening at the top of the cell were gone. Ezra gave a small shake of his head before walking toward the cell door and closing it. He didn't speak, he just gave me one final look before turning on his heels and disappearing down the dark hallway.

Nothing could be heard in the cell besides the faint breathing coming from Kai. I didn't expect him to say anything to me about what I said but if he did, I expected it to be nothing good. Things like he hated me, and he hoped my father killed me and let him go were they only words I could expect.

Leave it to Kai to do once again the unexpected. Instead of spewing hatred at me as anyone else would in this situation, instead he opened his mouth and said, "So, your dad seems like a fun time."

It was such a random thing to say and not the right time to make a joke, but that was him. It was in his nature to try to lighten the mood, to make others feel better in a situation where it seems like the only option is to be hopeless. In the short amount of time that I've known him, at least the times when I wasn't avoiding him, I couldn't help but keep a smile on my face. I thought it was because of the mark, but maybe that's just the type of person he was. That was the type of person I wanted to spend eternity with. I didn't care that he was as human, I didn't care what my father or the rest of my family thought. I wanted to be with him, and I was going to make that happen. We were both getting out of this cell alive.

I laughed or at least I tried to laugh. "You should try sitting through a dinner with him, you can really feel the familial bond."

Kai laughed, then the silence returned. "What now?"

A question I had no answer to, but I wasn't sure I wanted to admit that to him. It was bad enough I feared what was to come, I didn't want him to know that I was completely lost on how to get us both safely out of the situation I put us in. I had to tell him something though, so I said, "We're getting out of here of course." I couldn't see Kai's face, but I was really hoping my words sounded convincing to him because they didn't sound that way to me.

Before he could ask me to go into details on a plan I hadn't even formed yet, I placed both my hands flat on the cold, rough floor and made another attempt at dragging my body across the cell. There was one thing for certain, plan or no plan, I couldn't do anything until I fed.

I heard the rattling chains again but I didn't want Kai to hurt himself trying to get to me so I scooted faster, at least as fast as I could in this state.

By the time I made it to a point where I could barely reach his ankle, I was out of breath and drenched in sweat. They didn't just drain my blood to make me weak, they took me to almost the point of being comatose. Much longer without blood and my entire body would dry up and I would be essentially a living mummy, unable to move or speak.

Was that my father's plan? To turn me into that so my body was easier to dispose of, or did he plan to lock me away? Is that what he did to Cira? Turn her into a husk and then stash her away for when he needed a spare daughter? Now that I had disappointed him in the same way would he replace me with her now?

Kai slid his leg toward me, and his pants leg lifted, exposing a little of his bare ankle. My mouth instantly filled with saliva. As weak as I was, I could just barely make out the smell of his deliciously warm blood. It was so close, all I had to do was take one little bite and I would feel a hundred times better.

I reached for his ankle and leaned in. Just as my fangs lengthened so I could sink them into his skin, I heard the clanging of the cell door being opened and suddenly I was yanked away from Kai. With the force that was being used to drag me away combined with how weak I already was, I heard something snap, and an excruciating pain radiated from my hand all the way up to my shoulder. I screamed out in pain and tried to pull my arm away from the two guards that had rushed in, but I couldn't move it at all. Not because of how tightly they were holding it, but because I couldn't feel it. It must've broken when they grabbed me. Kai shouted my name but all I could give for reassurance was a whispered "I'm fine."

One of the guards let go of me long enough to pull another set of chains from the far opposite corner. He brought them over to me and got to work clamping one shackle to my wrist. The moment the metal touched my skin, I felt the sharp sting of my flesh melting. The sizzling could be heard loud and clear, then of course there was the unmistakable smell of burning meat and hair. Silver.

I flinched at the pain, and it took every ounce of strength not to scream out again, but I didn't want Kai to worry even more. One of us had to keep a level and focused head and with the amount of blood loss I was suffering from combined with a now broken wrist and burning flesh, I doubt it could be me.

The guards only released me when both my hands were shackled. Without them supporting my weight, my knees buckled, and I collapsed to the ground. They both turned to leave but not before I had a chance to ask them a question.

"Tell me what he's planning." I spoke with as much authority as I could manage. I may be a prisoner locked up in the basement of my own home, but this was still *my* home and these were *my* guards. Guards that have sworn to protect me since the day I was born. That had to mean something didn't it? It didn't. They didn't even bother to stop and face me. They left with no words.

They answered my question without answering my question. My father wanted the both of us dead, but now it was a matter of how it was going to be done. If I didn't have blood soon, I would be nothing but a husk, but what did they plan to do to Kai. My father's plan wouldn't be as simple as making us both starve. After what I've done, I knew he considered this the ultimate sign of disrespect. My father would want to punish me for that. Killing Kai wouldn't be enough. Drying me out wouldn't be enough. Ezra liked games and he loved to watch others suffer. There had to be more, I know there was.

"What now?" Kai asked. "You need blood and there's no way I can get it to you now."

He was right. I stared out the small window across the cell trying to come up with a new plan, but I was still having so much trouble focusing. The best I could come up with, regular conversation. Anything to take our mind off this tiny cell we were in.

"You aren't... angry?" I asked.

I heard a scraping sound, like he was adjusting his position. "Angry about what?"

"You have... every reason... to be angry." It felt like a sudden breeze came in through the window causing my whole body to shiver. There was silence, Kai didn't respond, and I was left to sit with my own thoughts. Of course, he would be angry, who wouldn't be. Mark or no mark, no one would be able to be forgiven after all of this.

If I had to guess how long we sat in this tiny box in silence, I would have to say two days had gone by since we were brought here. I've stared out that window for about that amount of time, watching the sun rise and set and rise and set again. In those two days Kai hadn't said one word to me. We'd sat in silence with the hardening of my bones the only sound I could hear. It wouldn't matter if Kai had spoken to me, my throat felt like sandpaper and now I've gotten to the point where I couldn't even produce saliva.

I couldn't move my legs anymore and the joints in my elbows were starting to stiffen. I'm surprised I was lasting this long, I thought for sure by now I would be reduced to nothing but a statue. Something was helping me hold onto myself and I wondered if it was Kai. The fact that he hadn't spoken to me in days and the last thing I asked him was about how much he hated me and never got an answer. Was that what was making me hold on? The thought that he might hate me, and I needed to hear him tell me maybe that was it.

I needed to know, but my body was past the point of being able to ask, instead all I could do was sit here and rot away. Maybe he would never tell me, and I would spend the rest of my existence never knowing, becoming a permanent part of this wall. That must be the way my father wants me to suffer.

I heard some scuffling coming from my left where the door of the cell was. I could no longer turn my head, but I figured it was the guards again, they had come by every couple of hours every day to check on us. They would bring Kai a small cup of water but no food. At night the cell would be freezing, under normal circumstances I would barely feel the cold but since I'd gone so long without consuming blood my entire body was deteriorating. Every part of me hurt and I couldn't even get my body to curl up into a ball to try and warm myself. Even during the day, because it was so dim in this cell, I couldn't see Kai clearly enough to check his condition and since he wasn't speaking to me and I could no longer talk, I couldn't ask him about it either.

I couldn't turn my head to see what the guards were doing. I expected them to just check to see if both of us were still separated but breathing and leave which had been their normal routine, but instead I heard the cell door clang open. A loud scuffling noise that sounded a lot like a bunch of feet running into the cell, but I couldn't see them. That is until I saw a dark figure make their way across the cell toward Kai.

I wanted to scream and warn Kai, but I couldn't open my mouth and even if I could, no sounds would come out. My body wouldn't move so there was no way I could stop them from attacking Kai. There was nothing I could do but sit here and watch what was going to happen next.

"My dear little willow, how I've missed you." My heart skipped a beat. I hadn't heard that name in decades. The person who spoke stood just out of view from me, but there was only one person who ever called me that.

That person unshackled the chains from my wrists and turned my body so I could look at them. My eyes swelled with tears as I recognized the strange but distinct silver streak that always graced the patch of hair that framed her face. A face I hadn't seen in a hundred years.

She wiped the tears that slid down my cheek. How strange, only moments ago I couldn't even produce saliva and now I couldn't seem to get the tears to stop flowing. "Don't cry little willow, we have a journey ahead of us and we must move."

Chapter 15

Those long flowing black and silver locks I use to love to play in when I was a girl. That soft smile that always told me no matter what I did, she could never not love me and those determined eyes that spoke volumes about the fiery passion that laid just below the surface. These were the things that made up my sister. My Cira. Someone I thought I would never get the chance to see again.

I opened my mouth to speak, but she stopped me. "Shh, there will be time for that later, right now we must leave." Cira grabbed one of my arms and raised her arm to motion for help. Another dark shadow appeared on my opposite side. They grabbed my other arm and with their combined strength, they managed to get me to my feet. I couldn't take my eyes off her. She was here with me again. Was the starvation I was suffering from making me delusional? Maybe I was having visions of my deepest desires, to be reunited with my sister. To have her rescue me just as she did all those years ago. To protect me from the man, we were forced to call our father.

Maybe I'd passed out and the guards had come in and finally put an end to my misery. This was heaven and I would get to spend the rest of eternity with my dear beloved sister Cira. The only suffering I would have was the knowledge that I could never be with Kai again. If I was dead and forced to never be allowed to see Kai again, would I be ok with that? Cira let go and suddenly I was scooped up into the mystery man's arms.

I still couldn't move my head so trying to find out if Kai was ok wasn't an option, I couldn't even call out his name. I guess I didn't need to say anything, the look on my face gave away exactly what I was thinking. "Don't worry, we have him." Cira leaned in and whispered in my ear before leading us out of the cell. I breathe a sigh of relief. We weren't just going to leave him behind at the mercy of my father and Laurel. Kai would be safe, that's all I cared about. That's all I've ever cared about.

The moment we walked out of the cell, I noticed there were no guards in sight. Did they abandon their posts or had my sister, and her men killed them. Was my Cira capable of something like that? A hundred years was a long time, people changed and if they planned on doing half the things I imagined to Kai and me, could I really blame her. Who's to say if I had the opportunity, I wouldn't have done the same.

The corridor was drafty, and I could hear water dripping from the ceiling into puddles that had gathered on the ground.

"This way" I heard Cira order. I wasn't sure how many men she brought with her, but I heard several sets of feet coming from behind me. She must have an army. I had so many questions running through my head. Where had she been this entire time? How did she know Ezra had locked me up? How did she get into the castle? So many questions, but she was right, this was not the time.

We maneuvered the dark, damp tunnels as quickly as we could but careful so as not to get separated. Down here, it was easy to get lost and if anyone got left behind, it would be nearly impossible to help navigate them out. The only reason Cira and I knew about these tunnels was because we use to love playing down here together when we were younger. You get lost down here a few times; you tend to pick up little tricks to help you find your way.

We were walking through the tunnels for I'm not sure how long, making a few lefts then a few rights. I was so tired, but it felt like if I went to sleep, I wouldn't wake up. Maybe if I just closed my eyes for a minute, I would feel better.

My eyelids got heavier and heavier by the second until they finally shut completely. I heard someone shouting but who was it? They sounded like they were giving demands, but underneath why did it seem like they were panicking? What were they afraid of, I was just taking a little nap that's it.

I felt my body shift, then the shivers were back. It was so cold.

"Niyla! Niyla!" Someone called out. "Niyla, you have to open your eyes!" Why? I was just resting my eyes. Just a second was all I needed.

She was so pale, so lifeless. Her skin was ice to the touch. From the distance we were apart in that cell I couldn't tell how bad she had gotten, but up close now I could see she was so much worse than I could've imagined.

"She needs blood!" shouted the girl with the two-toned hair. She seemed to be the leader of our group of *rescuers*. If you could even call them that. Yes, they broke us out of that cell, but I had no idea who she was or where she was taking us. For all I knew she could be taking us somewhere worse than where we came from. I didn't have much of a choice though, we had to get out of that cell if we had even the slightest chance of surviving and leaving with them seemed like the best course of action at the time.

They were so odd. They never spoke to me, they just stormed in, flooding the cell, and making it seem much smaller than we all knew it was. Unlocking my chains, they helped me to my feet and led us out. The only one of them I've heard speak until now was the girl. It was obvious that she knew Niyla, but that still didn't mean she could be trusted. For what I had witnessed about Niyla's father so far, he seemed like the type that liked to play mind games, so this whole thing could've been set up by him. Get our hopes up thinking that we'd escaped our prison only to snatch it all away.

I could hear the girl still arguing with one of the men. He wanted to keep moving, but just like me she thought it would be ok just to take a small break so that Niyla would have the time to feed. This was all background noise to me though, all I cared about was Niyla. We didn't have much time for her to explain the whole vampire thing to me. All we've been able to talk about so far was the giant circus that was her family. She never told me what happens to a vampire when they go for too long without feeding.

Her skin looked so thin, and it was obvious her bones were beginning to protrude from it. She was nothing but skin and bones and it hadn't even been that long since the last time she drank my blood. It had to be because they'd drained her the same day we got here. That's the only way she would deteriorate this fast right?

"You have to let her drink your blood." The girl said. She stood over my shoulder not taking her eyes from Niyla. "She's not allowed to drink from anyone else."

I turned to her; confusion written on my face. "Why?"

Her eyes met mine with probably the same amount of confusion on her face. "You are... marked, yes?" she asked. I didn't respond, instead I turned back to look at Niyla's pale face and nodded my head yes. Niyla did mark me. At the time I thought what she had done was a huge nuisance. Something that was going to throw off the plans I had set for my life. After a while, when I realized what it really meant, I thought it was something I could hate her for. What she had done to me put my life at risk and I should hate her for it, anyone else would. Oddly though, I couldn't bring myself to. The thought of someone harming her made the blood in my veins turn to ice and I didn't understand why I would feel so strongly about someone I had just met. Was that part of the deal when she put this mark on me?

"Has she not told you?"

"Told me what?"

The girl placed her hand on my shoulder causing me to look up and face her again. "An immortal who has marked a human cannot drink the blood of another human." I couldn't understand her words, so I waited for her to elaborate. "In other words, you human, are solely responsible for her survival."

What the hell does that mean? If she didn't drink my blood, she couldn't drink anyone else's? So, she would starve. My mouth hung open as I stared at the girl. I had so many questions I wanted to ask but I knew now wasn't the time for that, I had a sinking feeling in the pit of my stomach and only one question I needed an answer to at this very moment.

"If she never drank my blood again, what would happen to her?" The girl didn't need to say a word, instead all she did was motion toward Niyla's unconscious body.

That feeling in my stomach only intensified. So, my suspicions were right. Niyla planned on getting off my ship and disappearing from my life forever. She told me that eventually the bond from the mark would naturally fade over time and that my life would go back to how it was before she showed up. *My* life, she never said anything about what would happen to her if we separated, and I was too selfish to ask.

Was that really her plan? To disappear so she could die alone just so I could go back to the life I had before her.

"Cira." Someone called out. My head shot up at the sight before me. An older guy, dressed in all black wearing a shiny armored chest plate walked towards us. He placed his arm around the girl's waist pulling her close as if this was completely normal to them.

He called her Cira. Cira, as in Niyla's sister Cira. Is that who this young girl was? I guess, if I looked closely enough, I might be able to see some similarities, but how was she here. I suspected that she wasn't dead like Niyla had been told all those years, but I at least thought she might've been, locked away, somewhere that didn't allow her to return to Niyla's side.

I guess I was wrong. What doesn't make sense is why did she leave her all alone all this time?

I watched the man whisper something in Cira's ear before turning his attention back to me. "The guards have gathered, they're beginning their search on the tunnel, we have to keep moving."

"But my sister needs to feed." Cira protested. The man lifted his hand to her cheek and gently brushed it.

"We don't have the time my love. We will be back at the compound soon and then she will have plenty of time to feed." Cira seemed to immediately back down at his words which was shocking to me.

It didn't seem like there was much of anything that could make her submit, then again this is the same girl that had no problem abandoning her sister for all these years, maybe she just didn't care about her well-being as much as she claimed she did. If nobody else cared about her, I did, and if nobody else spoke up for her, I would.

"I'm not moving until she feeds." All eyes turned back on me. The man stepped away from Cira and took a step towards me. The men surrounding us mirrored his actions. Maybe they thought they could intimidate the poor weak human because they were a bunch of vampires, and I was nothing but a blood bag to them.

The man took another step towards me and crouched down, so he was eye level. I felt a vein in my forehead twitch at the action. I didn't like the fact that it seemed like he was talking to a spoiled child throwing a temper tantrum instead of a man defending the health of his woman. *My* woman.

"There is no need to be defensive, I was in your shoes once." That soothing tone he spoke in told me I was right; he saw me as nothing, but a spoiled child upset at not getting his way.

I narrowed my eyes at him. "Somehow, I doubt you've ever been close to my shoes."

He smirked and got to his feet. "We don't have much further to go and you can't give her enough blood in your condition. You haven't eaten in days, and you're dehydrated. Feeding her now would do nothing but kill the both of you."

I ground my teeth together because as much as I hated to admit it, he was probably right. In her condition, she more than likely needed way more blood than what I could produce right now. She would bleed me dry if what they said about her not being able to feed from another were true, if I died, she would die anyway.

Without saying another word, I got to my feet, scooping her in my arms along the way. I pressed her close to my body and felt her shiver. Her body felt even colder, and she was barely moving, it was almost like she was already gone. We needed to get to their little secret hide out and we needed to do it fast, I don't think she'll be able to last much longer.

Chapter 16

It seemed like we were walking forever and with every minute that passed, Niyla's condition only got worse. It had gotten so bad I was considering stopping again just to at least give her a few drops of my blood. Just enough to help her improve at least some, but every time I thought about it, that man would give me a look like he knew what I was thinking and then he would just shake his head at me, telling me I knew it wasn't the right move. I knew he was right, but that didn't stop me from contemplating it every time I felt her joints get stiffer, or every time her breathing got so shallow, I could barely hear it.

My legs were beginning to wobble, being in a dungeon for three days with no food and barely any water followed by a half-day trek through a maze of tunnels and a thick forest wasn't the most well thought out plan. I was out of breath and my stomach seized a few times, reminding me of just how empty it was. My tongue constantly stuck to the roof of my mouth and a few times my vision went blurry. I wasn't sure how much longer I could go on. It didn't help that I insisted on carrying Niyla this entire time. A few of the others offered to take her from me, but I refused to allow another man to touch her while I was still breathing. I was already contemplating how I could succeed in ripping Laurel's head off for thinking he could put his filthy lips on her.

"We're home." Came the man's voice. He walked up behind me and gave me a firm pat on the shoulder. "You did it." I hated how much I enjoyed his praise. An almighty vampire was praising me for being strong. It made me feel for just a second that I wasn't some useless human.

I followed him over a grassy hill, it took the last bit of energy I had to make it to the top, but once I did, I understood why they were so anxious to make it back. Tucked in at the bottom of the hill sat a compound. It was so hidden if I hadn't been looking for it, I never would've seen it. From the top it looked just like any other set of grassy, rolling hills, but the further down the hill we went the more the surprisingly large house began to reveal itself. A small stream of clear blue water sat right in the middle connecting one half of the compound to the other. Covered in grass and made of wood, one would think it would be old and run down but it was a well-kept and vibrant place, especially for this to be essentially a hide out. How their father had not found this place by now was a mystery to me. While Niyla and I were here, I could only hope it remained a mystery to him.

"Come, I'll show you where you can get some privacy, then we must talk." Cira led the way through a back entrance, away from the other men. She led us through what looked like a common living space to a door off in the corner. "This room should be good for the two of you. I'll have food brought to you soon so that you have the energy to feed my sister." Before I had a chance to ask any questions, or to even thank her for getting us out of that prison she turned her back to me and she was gone.

The room was small but cozy. A small full-size bed with a wooden bed frame sat in the middle. On one side of the bed, a rocking chair that also seemed to be made from wood. It had an intricate design carved into the back of it and what appeared to be a vine covered in leaves wrapping around the bars at the top. On the opposite side of the room sat a fireplace.

I walked around to the side of the bed and placed Niyla in the center. The bed was far from large but compared to how small she now looked; it seemed like it almost swallowed her whole.

I took a seat in the wooden chair, leaning forward and placing my hands on my knees. I did the one thing I was helpless to do for the last few days, I watched her. I had to watch her waste away to nothing until she was almost unrecognizable to the girl

I found hiding on my ship. The one I spent those nights locked in my room with. The both of us driving each other to new heights.

Knowing it was wrong but not caring all the same. This was the same girl, but it wasn't at the same time and now I had to sit here for how much longer while I waited to be brought enough food and water to give me enough energy just to let her feed from me. Until that happened, I had to continue what I had been doing, watching.

I sat for I'm not sure how long just watching the uneven rise and fall of her chest until I heard a light knock on the door followed by the doorknob turning. It was the man from earlier, the only one able to command these people besides Cira.

"I brought you food. It's not much but it should be enough to restore your strength." He sat a tray down on the edge of the bed in front of me. On it was a half loaf of bread, a small bowl of what looked like broth and some meat that smelled like chicken, but I wasn't entirely sure that's what it was.

The guy turned his head toward Niyla, and I could see sympathy in his eyes. I had a feeling that maybe I was wrong before, maybe he had been in my shoes once upon a time.

"She's going to need a lot from you." He spoke.

"I know that" I respond. I leaned over the tray he brought in and picked up the piece of bread. "She'll need my blood."

From the corner of my eye, I saw him shake his head. "That's not what I meant." He reached out and placed his hand on my shoulder. "She doesn't just need your blood; she has chosen to give up everything for you." I looked up to meet his eyes. I opened my mouth to argue that I didn't need him to tell me how much she was sacrificing for me, but the look on his face made me stop. He wasn't telling me this because he felt like he knew more than me and he could say something like this because he was with her sister, he was saying this because he had firsthand experience. This wasn't just some rescue mission he was on because it was the sister of the woman he was in love with. He

"Who are you?" I asked. He gave me a little smirk before looking back at Niyla.

"I'm you, a normal human man who fell in love with an immortal girl that needed rescuing." Turning back to me he gave a little shrug. "But you can call me Aris."

I couldn't mask the look of shock on my face. This was him, the man that was responsible for almost getting Niyla's sister killed. I shouldn't think of it like that, it was more like the guy she was willing to die for. It was just a speculation that Cira might still be alive, but I guess I never thought about if I believed her mate survived or not.

"Eat up." He spoke as he turned around and began heading toward the door. "She needs to feed as soon as possible and then we must strategize our next move." With those final words he disappeared, closing the door behind him and I was once again left alone with Niyla.

I knew I was hungry, but I guess I didn't realize just how bad it was until I had practically inhaled the plate of food that use to sit in front of me. Once the food was all gone, I wiped off my hands on my pants, kicked off my shoes and climbed into bed. Lifting Niyla up, I slid in behind her, resting her back on my chest and angling her neck. I pushed her head, so her lips pressed against the skin on my neck. A shiver ran down my spine, but Niyla didn't move. She was too weak to feed like this, so I had to figure something else out.

Glancing at the now empty tray that took my spot in the wooden chair, my eyes zeroed in on the small knife. It wasn't particularly sharp, but I was hoping it would get the job done. I shifted my body just enough to grab the knife. Holding it up to my wrist, I pressed the tip into my skin just enough to draw a single drop of blood.

The dark red liquid bubbled up, in my arms, I felt Niyla's body twitch almost like she could sense what was coming. I thought she might've been too out of it to sense my blood.

With that little bead of blood sitting on my arm, I held it up to her mouth and pressed it to her lips. For a moment, nothing happened, but then out of nowhere her arms lifted and her hands clamped tightly around my arm preventing me from moving. She opened her mouth wide, and I felt the sharp pierce of her fangs breaking through the skin and muscle of my wrist.

My arm twitched and my body stiffened but I tried not to move. I didn't want to interrupt her, I wanted her to take whatever she needed. With every pull of blood she took from my vein, it seemed like my body temperature increased four degrees. I tried to keep my desires in check, she was sick, and my blood was healing her, that's all. The more she drank the more it felt like the skin on my body was about to melt right off and the only way to stop it was to take her right here right now, but this wasn't the right time or place for that.

That's what I thought, other parts of me seemed to have other ideas though. I held her body close so she could comfortably drink from me, but the rise in her body temperature and the slow loosening of her muscles, softening of her skin and the pinkening change in her cheeks made certain parts of me rise to attention. What is wrong with me, she's weak and not even conscious and all I could think about was burying my face in those sweet thighs again. I wanted to make her feel good after everything she had been through. I wanted her to let go and not think about anything but the pleasure I was giving her at that moment.

That psychic link we had must've been working overtime because one second, I was looking down at her closed eyes as she suckled on my wrist and the next her eyes shot open. Blood red and mesmerizing to see. The first time I came face to face with these eyes was when she accused me of working with her father. Even though her words were supposed to be perceived as a threat, I couldn't help but remember how turned on I was at the way she looked at me. As angry as she was, I could still see the same burning desire in her eyes that I'm sure was reflected in mine.

This powerful, immortal being, just a few days ago laid underneath me, begging for me to make her release everything she had pent up in this small but oh so sexy body. I wanted to do it again. Niyla released her grip on my wrist instead turning and putting her hands on my shoulder, pushing me so I landed flat on my back. She threw her leg over me and positioned herself, so she straddled my hips. Without hesitation, she grabbed the edges on her T-shirt and pulled it over her head, exposing those beautiful breasts to my hungry eyes. Without hesitation, she leaned in and crushed her lips to mine. I groaned and tried to press my body closer to hers, reveling in the warmth and softness of her body. She felt so right in my arms. I reached between us and gripped her breasts, giving them a good squeeze. She let out a high-pitched moan and ground her core against my jean covered cock. She was going to make me bust, and I hadn't even taken my pants off yet.

I pushed her away slightly so I could tilt my head down and draw one of those delicious nipples into my mouth. I felt my cock jump at the feeling of having her sexy brown nipple between my lips. I pressed my lips together, giving the nipple a little squeeze. She moaned again running her hands through my hair and using her hips to press into my cock more. I wanted her legs around my head. I wanted to taste her. I *needed* to taste her, as much as I needed my next breath.

I pulled back from her, popping the buttons of her jeans. She rolled off me just long enough to pull them the rest of the way down before climbing back on top to straddle my hips. I smiled at her when I saw the look of desire clearly written in those bright red eyes. Her lips were still slightly tinted from the blood she drained from my wrist, but surprisingly, I wasn't disgusted by the sight in the least. On the contrary, it made me even more eager to drive her to ecstasy.

Reaching down, I hooked both my arms under each one of her thighs and pulled her towards me, placing her core so it was hovering right over my face. She gasped slightly but didn't try to fight me. Strange, considering how shy she was, I thought she would have something to say about this position. Instead, she looked down at me with half hooded eyes, her mouth hung open as she stuck out her tongue and licked her lips. Reaching behind her I popped the button of my jeans open and slid down the zipper to at least try to relieve some of the pressure. It only helped so much.

Niyla didn't need any more encouragement; she lowered her hips, so her sweet pussy landed right on my waiting tongue. I couldn't help but groan when I tasted her on my tongue, my hips bucking involuntarily. My aching cock wishing that it could be the one to feel these tight muscles wrapped around it. I flicked my tongue against her slit and enjoyed the moans that came from her parted lips.

She tasted just as good as she did the last time I was between these thighs. I started with slow leisurely strokes of my tongue with little flicks once I got near her little bundle of nerves. The louder her moans got, the faster I licked, making sure to lap up every drop of that delicious cream that flowed from her. Her lips rocked against my face, and I let her pick the tempo, going at whatever speed and pressure she wanted me to. It wasn't long before her hips began bucking and the moans came one after the other. Niyla leaned forward and placed her hands flat on the bed over my head and rode my face to completion, screaming my name as she did.

Her body convulsed and spasmed until finally her muscles went limp. Licking her juices from my lips, I rolled her off me and pulled her into my arms. I noticed that her eyes had changed back to that gorgeous grey color just before she closed them. I spent the rest of the night listening to her soft breathing as she slept.

So warm, I haven't felt this warm in what seemed like forever, what was it? I snuggled in closer; I couldn't get enough of this feeling. I felt like I would die if I let this warmth get away.

Suddenly that big, soft, warm cloud that had just provided me with so much comfort moved. My eyes shot open, and I surveyed my surroundings. The panic that set in was instant, I had no idea where I was. I tried lifting my arms but they both felt like they weighed a million pounds. My legs, even heavier.

"Are you finally awake?" A voice I would know anywhere. One I had missed hearing and for a second, I was worried I would never hear again.

Luckily, it seemed like I at least had control over my head, so I was able to lift it enough to look into those overwhelming blue eyes. Kai.

I breathed a sigh of relief when I saw him. He was here, we were together and if what I could see of this room was any indicator, we had made it out of the castle.

I stuck my tongue out to moisten my lips before I spoke. "Where are we?" My voice sounded rough to my ears, but at least it wasn't as difficult to speak as it was before.

"We're safe." Was his response as he gave me a smile that gave me the impression, he was relieved that I was up and talking. I can only imagine how I must've looked to him rotting away in that prison, but we had gotten out and since I was starting to feel better that must mean he had given me some blood.

"I had such a strange dream." I snuggled in closer to him, enjoying every ounce of warmth his body provided mine.

I felt Kai's chest rumble as he let out a little chuckle. "A dream huh?"

"I was wasting away in that prison. I thought we were going to die but then, my sister was there." I closed my eyes, trying to hold tightly to the vivid dream. "She was there to save me just like when we were kids."

Kai lifted his hand to brush hair from my cheek. "Is that all you dreamed about it?" He asked. I opened my eyes and craned my neck to look at him.

"What do you mean?" Kai pulled the blanket we had draped over us back to reveal that I was completely naked. I gasped and tried to cover myself.

"You don't remember anything?" I shook my head no. "What is the last thing you do remember?"

"I remember the cell and somehow we escaped. I had a dream that Cira was there. That she helped us." Kai speculated that my sister might still be alive, but I know that if she had been all these years, she would've come for me. There's no way my sister is in this world anymore.

"It wasn't a dream sweetheart. Your sister Cira, her and her men came for us. They are the ones who got us out." I stared at him for what seemed like an eternity, just letting his words rattle around in my head. I replayed his sentence repeatedly *your sister came for you.* That couldn't be right. Before I could ask him anymore questions, I heard the loud creak of old wood under pressure. I turned my head, yanking the blanket up to cover my chest just in time to see someone walk into the room. Someone I shouldn't be seeing, someone that shouldn't be alive.

"You're awake little willow." That soft smile she gave me brought tears to my eyes instantly. It wasn't a dream, she was here, my sister had come back to save me. I did my best to lift my free arm as far as I could, reaching for her. Cira didn't hesitate to cross the room and pulled me into her arms, holding me tight. "I've missed you too little willow."

I inhaled her sent. She smelled the same, like flowers and something sweet. She smelled like home. Cira pulled away from me, brushing away a stray tear from my face.

"There will be time for our reunion later, right now we are having an emergency meeting in the main hall, and we would like the two of you to join us." She took a step away from the bed looking at the both of us.

"A meeting about what?" Kai asked. "You've helped us escape right, so it's over and we can leave."

Cira shook her head no. The look of pity on her face caused a sense of dread to overtake me. "This is far from over; Ezra won't stop until he has one or both of us under his control. She turned her eyes toward me. "This isn't up for debate, if you want your mate to survive, Ezra has to go."

Chapter 17

I sat on Kai's lap, and he held me close as the surprisingly large group of people started filing into the main room. There was a large table in the center, on one side sat Kai and I, right across from us Cira and the man I now knew as Aris, Cira's mate. There were about eight other men that filled in the rest of the space around the table and too many to count sat on some of the couches that surrounded us.

I noticed everyone in the room wore such strange clothing, including Cira and her mate. They were all dressed in dark green cloth, some of them wore black armor plates on their chests, black boots and even weapons were strapped to their backs. Some swords, I think I even saw a few battle axes. This wasn't just a community of people living in the woods outside the castle's grounds together, this was an army that seemed to be commanded by my sister.

The room was filled with the mumbles of everything that was going on. I heard a few whispers about there being another human on the compound. Some whispers about Cira coming to rescue me and even a few excited mumblings about killing my father. I wasn't sure how I felt about that. Did I really want Ezra dead?

Cira got to her feet, drawing everyone's attention to her. "Everyone, I need your attention." The room grew quiet. Their eyes glued as they hung on every word she said. This was the power my sister had acquired since leaving home.

"There has been a great development." Cira turned to look at me. "My sister and I have been reunited." I heard a few gasps followed by more whispers and many people turned their eyes to stare at me. "I've been trying for a long time to get my sister back and now that I've done it, there's nothing stopping us from moving forward with our plan." She stuck out her chest and stood proudly before her people. This didn't seem like the same sister I remembered from all those years ago. Before, my Cira was strong yes, but she would never hurt anyone. She wanted nothing more than to be free to paint the beautiful portraits she use to make for me and be the dutiful daughter my father use to be proud of. Everything had changed now. Is this what loving someone can turn you into?

"You're not serious about killing your father, are you?" All eyes turned to Kai except mine. Our bond was still going strong, so I knew we both wanted an answer to the same question. Instead, my eyes remained locked on Cira. I held my breath in anticipation of her answer.

"This isn't a joking manner human." She responded. "Ezra has wreaked havoc over our people and especially our family for hundreds of years all in the pursuit of power, he needs to be stopped. After what he has done to you and my sister, you should want this as well."

After all the horrible things he had done to me over the centuries, she was right, I should want him dead. He tried to kill my mate, that alone should make me want to remove his head from his shoulders, but he was still the only father I've ever known. Could I really be a part of his demise?

"Remember sister, he is the one who has kept us apart for all these years." Cira's words drew my attention. "There was a reason I hadn't been able to come back to you sooner and his name is Ezra Grey." I stared at her in confusion. I had no idea what she meant by that. Did he do the same thing to her that he did to me or was it something more.

Kai and I chose not to interrupt her anymore, so she went back to addressing her army. "For years, we've all agreed not to make any moves against Ezra until my sister was safe and now that she is, there is nothing stopping us from moving against my father... tomorrow." Tomorrow? She couldn't be serious. It just wasn't possible to plan a way to kill my father and act on it so quickly.

Kai and I sat there quietly listening to the different plans they had all strategized after all these years. There were about three different versions of this plan, a through c. The first was straightforward, use the tunnels we used to escape to sneak back into the castle, disabling the guards and cutting off any escape routes for Ezra. Plan B was to use the guard they had on the inside to do a single man attack, destroying my father while he unknowingly slept. The last plan which, in my outsider opinion, was the most drastic, was burning down the entire castle with everyone inside. Guards, blood slaves, servants and even our mother, she didn't care about harming any of them.

The meeting broke up not long after they finalized each soldier's individual roles and the signals needed in case something had to be changed at the last minute. Kai and I remained in our seat with Aris and Cira sitting together on the opposite side of the room after the rest of the room had cleared out. I didn't know what to say to her. This was my sister, my Cira, who I hadn't seen in so long. I should be over the moon to have her back in my life. I should be thrilled that her and her mate are together despite my father's actions. What I should be doing is catching up with her. Telling her how I rebelled against Ezra at my birthday party and stowed away on Kai's ship. In return she would tell me how her and Aris met and fell in love. These are the types of things that long lost sisters should be discussing but right now all I could think was who was this person with my sister's face.

"I hope you aren't angry about my decision." Cira said. She rubbed her hands together nervously and adverted her eyes to look everywhere but at me. She was like a completely different person compared to the woman I just witnessed commanding her army.

"Cira, it is clear I cannot stop you from doing this, but I'm not sure I can be a part of it. Sorry excuse for a father or not, he is still our father."

Cira shook her head at me. "You say that because you don't know what he has done." Aris reached over and wrapped his arm around her shoulders. I watched as he used his thumb to rub small, soothing circles on her arm.

"She should know so that she can understand." I stared at Aris in confusion. I had no idea what either one of them was talking about. Ezra had used Laurel to track Kai and I down, bled me dry, and locked us in a cell for days waiting for the two of us to die. I can't imagine what he did to us being that different from what he probably did to them. Yes, it was horrible to have something like that done to you, especially by the man that's supposed to love and protect you no matter what, but wouldn't the best course of action be to run. We could disappear, why wasn't that an option for her.

"What aren't you telling me?"

Cira shook her head, still refusing to make eye contact with me. "You're still weak little willow, you should feed again so that you can rest."

I heard a small crack in her voice when she spoke. She was hiding something from me, and I wasn't giving up until she told me what it was. "That's not going to work Cira, I want to know what happened and I want to know now." If I was expected to help kill my own father, I deserved to know everything.

"You don't make demands here princess." Aris chimed in, giving me an annoyed look in defense of my sister.

Kai got to his feet so quickly, I stumbled and almost lost my balance. He pushed me behind him and took a step forward. "And you don't talk to her that way."

"Enough!" Cira shouted, slamming her hand on the wooden table. I flinched, grabbing Kai's sleeve, and pulling him back a little. Cira's fangs were showing, and her eyes were glowing red as she lifted her head to look at me. Just as quickly as the signs of her anger were there, they disappeared.

"It is my story to tell, and she is right, she should know the extent of our dear father's cruelty." Though her fangs had retreated, and her eyes were back to normal, I could still hear the venom dripping in her words. It wasn't directed at us, no, this was her hatred for Ezra.

Kai sighed and ran his hands through his hair before re-turning to his seat and grabbing my arm to pull me back into his lap. He held me tightly but kept his eyes locked on Aris almost like he was daring him to make a move in our direction. Aris hesitated before taking his seat as well. It was too much testosterone in this room right now, so I was beyond thankful when Cira opened her mouth to speak again.

"Years ago, Aris use to be confined to the palace as one of our blood slaves. He was assigned to me specifically." Cira kept her eyes trained to a spot on the table. I could feel my eyes grow wide. I wasn't expecting that, I thought maybe Cira had met Aris at one of the shipping ports or maybe she had made it off the island and met him that way like I did. I never would've imagined Cira mating with a blood slave.

She looked up at me. "You looked shocked sister. Never thought I would stoop low enough to fall in love with a blood slave?"

"That's not it, I just assumed when father let you off the island for your year away, you met him then."

Cira exchanged a look with Aris before she leaned back in her chair and ran a hand through her hair. "You really are so naïve little sister. That year off Ezra promised you, was nothing more than another one of his lies. He told you that to garner compliance and I bet you gave him every little bit of it. He once promised me the same but when it came time for me to leave, I was suddenly looking into the eyes of someone he had chosen for me to marry."

My heart skipped a beat. The year away was a ruse. How did I not see that? Suddenly all the questions Kai had asked me about the arrangements my father had made, made complete sense. I didn't know the information because there was no information to know.

He had asked me why I would believe my father would let me go that easily and I should've listened then.

"Since I was betrothed already thinking about falling for someone else never even crossed my mind." She lifted her head to look into Aris's eyes. "I couldn't help it though; he was always there to make me laugh and a shoulder to cry on when Ezra was being too... well Ezra." I watched as a smile broke the serious look on Aris's face. He leaned in to kiss her forehead. "It was hard not to fall in love with him and as you've figured out, that's strictly forbidden.

We kept it secret as best we could, but somehow, we were still found out. To this day, I'm still not sure who it was that told Ezra," Cira let out a frustrated huff before continuing her story. "Nevertheless, he found out.

One night while I was sleeping, a bunch of guards came into my room and snatched me from my bed. I woke up in a cell with Aris just like you." Cira squirmed in her seat. I was aware that telling me all of this was probably making her uncomfortable, but I needed to know.

"We were down there for days until my body turned to stone just like yours almost did." So far, our stories sounded the same, but there was something I was clearly missing so I waited patiently for her to finish.

"Fortunately for us, there were still guards that were more loyal to me than they were afraid of Ezra. They freed us and brought us here. There was already a small revolution against Ezra's power brewing, and they had decided we would be the perfect ones to lead it."

I lifted my head to look into Kai's eyes and that's when I realized he shared the same confused look that was probably written all over my face. "There's something you're leaving out isn't there?" Kai spoke for both of us.

It looked as though Cira was holding back tears, so instead of answering Kai's question, she remained quiet, and Aris answered for her. "By the time the guards had come to help us escape, it was too late, the damage had already been done?"

"What damage?" I asked, turning back to them, none of this was making sense.

Aris let out a sigh before answering. "Cira was pregnant, she had found out a few days before we were locked away." It felt like all the air rushed out of my lungs. I knew where this story was going but I wasn't sure I wanted to hear them say it.

"What does that mean?" Kai asked. As a human who didn't grow up anywhere near this island or around immortals, of course none of this would make sense to him.

I tightened the grip I had on the hand he held around my waist. Turning my head back to him, I place a soft kiss on his lips. A tear slipped from my eye as I stared into his deep blue ones. "When an immortal starves, everything turns to stone and for females that includes the womb. A child would never be able to survive that. Ezra killed their child."

Chapter 18

Laying in this bed, staring at the dark brown ceiling with Kai's arms wrapped tightly around me, I couldn't get my mind to shut off. I couldn't stop thinking about what Cira told me. She had been pregnant and because of what Ezra had done to her, they had lost a child. I asked to be told everything, but now I don't know what to do with that information. Should I hate him for what he had done to my sister and almost did to me, or should I give him the benefit of the doubt and hope that he didn't know about her condition at the time. Even hoping that he just didn't know didn't make what he did any better.

I didn't like feeling like this, like I'm being pulled in two different directions, and I can't decide because I don't know what happened. I needed to talk to Ezra before it was too late. Shifting my body a little, I tried my hardest to slip out of Kai's grasp without waking him up. He couldn't come with me, I refused to put him back in harm's way so bringing him before my father just wasn't an option.

Luckily before we both went to bed, I was able to feed from Kai again, which meant I was for the most part back to 100%. Kai groaned at all my movements then rolled over in the other direction, releasing me. I breathed a sigh of relief and quickly climbed out of the bed, using my speed to make it out of the room before he had a chance to notice. The rest of the compound was quiet except for a few men sitting out front guarding.

I snuck out through the back, trying my hardest to maneuver through the thick bushes and trees without so much as snapping a branch. The guards were immortal just like me so they would be able to hear everything. I couldn't afford to get caught before I got some answers.

When I felt like I was far enough away, I used my speed to get me the rest of the way. What would've been a day and a half of a walk, I knocked down to maybe about an hour. I couldn't waste any time, I had to be back before anyone noticed.

When the castle grounds came into view, I stopped. Oh, how I hated this place. Maybe burning it down wasn't the worst idea. I made my way through the maze of the surrounding foliage somehow managing to avoid any guards. Which was strange, there seemed to be a lot less guards surrounding the castle than there usually was. I found a rock underneath one of the lower windows and used it to break the glass before climbing through. Even with all that noise, not one guard showed up. Where was everyone?

I looked around the room and realized I was in the library. I used to love this place, as big as it was, I use to love coming here when I was a child to hide from my parents. Now wasn't the time to reminisce, I needed to find my father. Scurrying across the large room I made it to the door, but just as I was about to reach for the doorknob, it suddenly flew open and on the other side stood my mother.

The almighty Lilianna Grey, absolutely the last person I wanted to see right now. Her long chocolate brown wavy hair with the one white streak in it just like Cira, hung loose just like always. Appearance wise, she looked just as young as me and my sister, if you didn't know any better one would guess she was no more than 18 herself.

"Welcome home daughter, your father and I have been expecting your arrival." She spoke. The smile on her face was sickeningly sweet, one I use to hate when I was a child. My mother was just as cruel as my father, maybe more so because she never lifted a finger to stop him from tormenting us. "Come, he is waiting for us." She ushered me out of the library and into the room across the hall, my father's study.

She opened the door and pushed me into the room. "Ezra my dear, she has arrived." The dark brown wood paneling on all the walls, the marbled floors, the desk that was much too big to make sense in this room and my father sitting right behind it. His fingers laced together, and he wore a smirk on his face. My mother closed the door behind us and took a seat on the sofa to my right.

Ezra got to his feet and slowly walked around the desk, leaning back against it. He wore a white loosely fitted shirt that was only buttoned halfway and black slacks. His shiny black dress shoes echoed on the marbled floors when he walked. "Welcome back Niyla. I was so worried when you disappeared." I rolled my eyes. He could never stop with the mind games, could he?

"Are we really going to play this game again Father?"

He chuckled. "No, no of course not, but I am curious. Tell me why you came back?"

"There's something I need to know."

My mother laughed, crossing one leg over the other. "What makes you think we are obligated to answer anything you have to ask."

I turned to face her and said, "Because I deserve it, so this time, you don't get to ask the questions, I do." Before turning back to Ezra. I crossed my arms and stared him down. I was starting to feel like I was on trial and if I said the wrong thing it could be very dangerous.

Ezra's calm, annoyingly giddy face immediately split into one of anger. His eyes turned red, his nails turned into claws, and he bared his fangs at me.

"Do not speak that way to your mother Niyla." Though he appeared to be furious with me, he still spoke so calmly.

"Why?" I asked. After years of them doing this to me, making me feel small and insignificant, I refuse to allow either one of them to intimidate me anymore. "I do not need to show her, or you respect if you do not respect me. It is only fair."

He gave me a smirk, but it appeared a lot more vicious than I think he intended considering his fangs were still out. "Niyla, I will not have much more of your attitude. Now tell me what this is about." He sounded like he was on the brink of losing his temper. If he was willing to fake the death of one daughter and attempt to kill the other, I wouldn't put it past him to rip my throat out just for angering him.

"Why didn't you tell me Cira was still alive?"

In the blink of eye, my father's face returned to normal. "I saw no need to. She was dead to this family, that's all that mattered."

"You can't expect me to take that as a satisfactory answer."

"You forget yourself Niyla." He turned his back to me, walking around the desk and returning to his seat, leaning forward, and placing his elbows on his desk. "I do not owe you an explanation for anything I do. I never have and I never will. Your sister chose a pathetic human over her family, and she paid the price for that." What the hell did that mean? Was that his way of confessing to knowing exactly what he was doing when he locked Cira away?

This was the man that raised us, but it always seemed as though he never really cared about us, only what we could do to help this family's power grow nothing more nothing less. If you aren't useful, he'll toss you aside, blood or not. "Were you ever going to tell me?"

He waved his hand at me almost like he was shooing me off and sat back in his chair. "As I said there was no need to, she was dead to this family." That was all the confirmation I needed. The man I considered my father, the one who I thought would at least love and protect me and not just control me, he was dead to me. Whatever Cira had planned for him, it was clear he deserved every bit of it.

"That was all I needed to hear. Thank you for your time, Ezra." I gave him a slight bow and turned on my heels to leave.

"One more thing before you leave daughter." Ezra called out. Something about the way he said the word *daughter* sent a shiver down my spine, but I turned around to face him. This would be the final words I ever heard from him so I might as well listen. "You've been rebellious over the years, ever since you were a child, but I've never considered you foolish until just this moment."

"What are you talking about?" He had my full attention now. Coming here alone might've been foolish but somehow, I don't think that's what he was talking about.

"Oh, come now my darling daughter, did you really think escaping that cell would've been possible unless I allowed it?" I suddenly felt sick to my stomach. He couldn't mean what I thought he did. It was a set up.

"You and that human you so irresponsibly marked led me right back to your sister and her little gang of resistance." No, there's no way this entire thing was a set up. "If that's not foolish enough, you then chose to leave that same mate all alone and completely defenseless." Ezra poked his bottom lip out and did his best impression of someone sad and pouting.

I felt all the air rush from my lungs. My heart was suddenly racing. I had to get back to Kai, he needed me. I raced to the door and tried to yank it open, but it didn't budge.

"Leaving so soon?" He asked. "If you're rushing back to see your precious human, you're too late he's already gone."

I turned back to face him, I'm sure the horror was evident on my face. "You're lying!" I shouted at him. He had to, there was no way he could get to Kai, not with my sister and her people protecting him.

"Now Niyla, you know lying is the one thing that I will never do."

"Untrue, you've been lying to me my entire life. Why should I believe anything you say now?"

"By all means, if you don't believe me, you're free to go." He waved his hand toward the door. I turned and grabbed it cautiously, prepared for the worse. I turned the knob slightly and with a small click the door popped open.

Opening the door all the way, I took a step out into the hallway but before leaving I turned back to face my parents. They hadn't moved from their spots, my mother was still sitting on the sofa and my father behind his desk. Both looked completely calm and relaxed, like it was no big deal to threaten someone's life, an innocent.

If they could threaten, so could I. "If anything happens to him, neither of you will be safe."

"Funny, your sister made a similar threat, yet here we are, stronger than ever." I was done listening to them, I needed to get back to Kai, I needed to prove that they were lying, and he was completely fine.

I don't know how I managed it, but I was able to cut the amount of time it would've taken to get back to the compound in half. I had no time to lose, the closer I got to the compound the more the dreed sunk in. It was like my body knew something was wrong, but I couldn't seem to get my brain to admit it, I had to see it for myself.

When I got close enough to see the small main house, I knew instantly there was something wrong. No guards, and it was much too quiet. Now that the sun was high in the sky, I expected there to be a lot of activity inside but there was nothing. I needed to get closer.

I crossed through the rest of the bushes until I was standing right in the middle of the compound, there was no one around. Looking around, I took in everything. It was eerily quiet, almost like everyone just disappeared. I took off running back to the main hall where I left Kai sleeping. When I reached it, the door was wide open, and the bed was empty. My heart sank to the bottom of my chest.

Unlike everywhere else on the compound, this room showed signs of a struggle. The bed was torn to shreds, blankets, and pillows everywhere. A pillow lay in the fireplace where just a few hours ago a warm fire heated up the room we slept in. The small wooden chair was in pieces scattered all over the floor and even the window above the bed was shattered. I wasn't sure if I should feel better or worse that Kai didn't go quietly, he put up a fight. I didn't smell his blood, so I had to be hopeful that he was still alive.

Walking over to the bed, I sat on the edge, rubbing the spot his warm body use to lay. This was my fault, why couldn't I have just stayed away from him. The plan I had to disappear from his life and die on my own, why couldn't I have just done that. My eyes filled with tears as I stared at the spot, imagining he was still there. I used my free hand to furiously wipe my eyes, I could cry later, right now I had to find him.

I got to my feet and headed to the door, I had no plan and no idea how I was going to get him back. Maybe the mark could help, maybe it couldn't, but there was no way I was going to leave him to Ezra's will. Speaking of Ezra, my mind was so busy reeling at Kai's disappearance, I completely missed detecting his little minion's presence. Laurel now stood in the doorway leading outside, staring at me with that infuriating smirk.

"Lovely home you have here." His eyes traveled around the room before landing back on me.

I stalked towards him, ready for a fight if one was called for. "Cut the bullshit, I want him back and I want him back now." I was sick of all these games. I was tired of being a pawn, I was tired of the lying and I was tired of fighting for everything I wanted. The days of me playing the dutiful daughter to Ezra were over. Weak little Niyla, who needed everyone else to take care of her was gone. Now, I want blood.

"I see being around this human has taught you to forget your manners, but that's ok. I'll forgive you this once. In fact, being the loving fiancé that I am, I'll even return the human to you on one condition.

"What do you want?" I folded my arms across my chest and eyed him suspiciously.

"Simple. Mate with me and all will be forgiven."

Chapter 19

"I'll make sure your little human friend is returned to his old life; all you must do is marry me. It's just that simple." He couldn't be serious about this. He helped my father to do all this just to get me to marry him.

"I want to know where Kai is." I needed to see him, and I didn't have time to play any games with this narcissist.

"Oh, don't worry, he's safe... for now." I couldn't trust anything he said, and I couldn't sense Kai. I wasn't sure why, but the ability to fully sense Kai, or even hear his thoughts had yet to manifest. My eyes traveled around the room, silently wishing none of this was real. That I wasn't foolish enough to leave the safety of the compound just to confront Ezra. I left my mate and the sister I was finally reunited with all because I chose to have faith in the same man who chose to lock me up instead of letting me be happy. I should've believed my sister's words.

Maybe I wouldn't have been able to stop the attack, but at least I would've been with them.

"Agree to be my wife." He commanded.

"You say it like you're giving me a choice in the matter." There was no choice, there was do this or there was no chance of ever seeing the ones I love ever again.

"Well, you don't, but" Laurel crossed the room so that he could stand in front of me. He lifted his hand up to gently rub my cheek with his cold knuckle. I jerked my head away. I didn't want anyone but Kai to touch me and it made me sick to my stomach that he believed he was entitled to do it. "It would be nice if you were my wife willingly."

"And why the hell would I do anything for you after you kidnap my mate and hid him from me." I didn't see the slap coming, suddenly, the entire left side of my face was on fire. My head whipped to the side, and I lost my balance, falling to the wooden floor.

"That weak human is not your mate. You are betrothed to me, and I am to be your mate remember that."

The metallic taste of my blood filled my mouth. I spit the dark red liquid out before looking up at him. "He's already my mate, that can't be changed."

Laurel stood up straight, looming over me. To me he always seemed like the type that loved to intimidate those smaller than him, just like Ezra. "There are ways around that. All you must do is convince him that you want this wedding."

"But I don't." I would rather stake myself than let this creatin mark me.

Laurel's face didn't change. The same arrogant look remained. "That doesn't matter, you must convince him that you do. Think about his safety. Don't you think he should be with his own kind. Someone he can have a normal life with." I looked away from him, I didn't want him to see my face and know that as much as it sickened me to my stomach, he was right. Kai could never have a normal life with me. Besides having to feed from him just to survive, there was also the chance that I would never be able to get rid of Ezra and Laurel, so was I expecting him to spend the rest of his life looking over his shoulder, wondering if they would take him away again? Torture him and maybe even kill him. That wasn't the life he deserved, it was the life I was forcing on him and that wasn't fair to him. If I really loved him, then maybe it would be best to let him go back to his ship, a place where he was the happiest.

I would let Kai go and with that realization, I felt a tear slide down my cheek. Laurel reached down and grabbed my chin, yanking my head to face him. He saw my tear-stained face and smiled the biggest smile.

"I see you've made your decision." He let go of my face but made sure to scratch it slightly with one of his claws when he did. I instantly felt the blood drip down to my chin. "Once all the arrangements are made, you'll get your final chance to see him."

I stared straight ahead at the back of his legs as he walked towards the door. "I want to see my sister."

He didn't turn around to face me when he responded. "She's already waiting for you back at the castle. I heard she's giving the guards a hard time so you might want to hurry back. Wouldn't want anything bad to happen to her." In a flash he was gone, and I was left alone with my thoughts.

I couldn't believe what I had just agreed to. In short, I was selling my soul to the devil, or should I say *devils.* But what choice did I have, it was all for the safety and happiness of the person I loved. If I had to suffer for eternity just so he could be happy then that's what I would do. Kai was all that mattered, so no more fantasizing about escaping and running away and being together forever. To make sure he survived this, I was going to have to break both of our hearts.

I sat there, silently staring at the tiny swirls on the hardwood floors for so long, the wounds on the outside of my cheeks as well as the cut on the inside had already begun to heal. I couldn't sit and wallow forever. The sooner I got back to the castle to make sure Cira wasn't harmed, the faster I would at least feel a little better about the situation I had found myself in.

It didn't take me long to make it back to the castle but unlike before, all the guards were back at their regular posts. None of them tried to stop me as I confidently walked right through the front door. Though I might be sick to my stomach and hating every minute of being back in this place, I refused to let anyone else see me weak. They would all view me as the strong, untouchable vampire that I wasn't.

When I got to my room, there were two big, burly guards standing outside of the door. One bald with a scar going across his left eye, the other had dark hair braided to the back. Neither one of them looked at me when I approached, they both just stepped away from the door so I could enter.

As soon as I opened the door I was immediately yanked into the room, the door was slammed shut and I was thrown up against it. All the air rushed from my lungs, but I quickly recovered. I was just about to fight back when I realized that it was Cira who was strong enough to pin me to the door.

"Cira?" There was a shocked look on her face before she released me, and I slid down the wall landing on my feet.

"Sorry, I thought you were one of the guards."

I rolled my shoulders to try and help reduce some of the ache I was feeling from being slammed into the thick wood.

Cira took a step away from me and began pacing the room. I kind of thought she would be a little happier to see me. "You aren't surprised to see me?" I asked. I know I was surprised when Laurel told me that she wasn't locked away as well. Why didn't they lock her away with Kai and Aris? It didn't make sense; she was one of the leaders of the resistance so she should be locked away with them.

"Cira, what are you doing here?" She stopped pacing to face me.

"What do you mean? Your guess is as good as mine." She ran her hand through her thick dark mane. That one patch of white still so prominent mixed in with the rest of her hair.

I closed the distance between us and grabbed her hands. She was shaking. It probably unsettled her to be away from Aris, I was feeling the same being away from Kai.

"What happened?"

She looked away from me, like the memory was too painful to think about. "They came while we slept. There were so many of them and so few of us, they overpowered us." Cira hesitated before finishing. She chewed on her bottom lip and turned back to face me. "They destroyed everyone. Drove a streak through every single one. The three of us were the only ones to survive." That sick feeling came back. My father wasn't just ok with torturing humans, he was also perfectly fine with killing his own kind just because they had gotten in his way. There were families there. I had even seen a few small children. They tried to keep them out of sight when it came to planning war strategies, but they were there and they were innocent. Were they also causalities in that attack?

"Where is Kai?" I asked. If they were willing to kill immortal children, why would I think they would keep their word about keeping some insignificant human safe?

Tears formed in Cira's eyes. "I don't know, they separated us. They brought me here and I don't know where they took either of them or what they want from us. This seems like more than just trying to stop us from fighting back against Ezra's rule."

Cira began quietly mumbling to herself, trying to make different connections that would explain what Ezra's plan was. Why he wouldn't just kill them just like the others and why would he separate her from her mate again. She was lost in her own little world, and I couldn't do anything but stare at her while she came up with millions of different conspiracy theories. The truth is, after all these years spent living under this man's thumb, neither one of us had any clue what he was capable of.

I let go of her arms, walking around her and sitting on the edge of my bed. "Cira, this is all about that ridiculous marriage that Ezra wants from me."

She had stopped mumbling when I spoke. "What marriage?" I guess whatever spies she had in the castle hadn't told her everything.

I let out a sigh before going into the explanation. I didn't want to think about it because there was no way I was going through with it. Even if I said I would marry Laurel, I've already marked Kai. That mark is permanent, I can't mark someone else. I can't even consume the blood of someone else. "Ezra wants me to marry one of his generals to help strengthen the family. Some nonsense he tried to feed me. I didn't believe him, I know exactly why he wants me to marry him, because it's just another way he can con-"

"What's his name?" Cira interrupted me. She rushed to me, crouching down and grabbing my hands, forcing me to look her in the eyes.

"Why does that matter?"

She yanked my arms and got closer to my face. "I'm serious, tell me his name." The way she was looking at me told me just how desperate she was for me to give her an answer, but why?

"Laurel. His name is Laurel." Cira let me go and quickly got to her feet. My eyes followed her as she went back to pacing around the room. Her boots scraping the marbled floors as she moved rapidly back and forth, tugging at her hair and looking like she was struggling to mentally put pieces together. Her eyes stayed glued to the floor while her mind seemed to be racing a mile a minute.

"He's still trying it. After all these years, I thought after he couldn't get me to go through with it, he would let it go." I had no idea what she was talking about and for just a second, I thought she might've forgotten I was even there since she seemed to be so caught up in her own thoughts.

"What's going on? Do you know Laurel?" I asked. She didn't respond, she just continued to pace. I was sick of this. Why did it seem like at every turn this family was keeping something from me. First it was the fact that I was even promised to someone in the first place, then it was that Cira had been alive after all these years. If that isn't bad enough now, I'm finding out my own father has some hidden agenda that involves me marrying the most detestable immortal on probably the entire planet and to make it worse I don't even know what the agenda was.

This is ending right now. "Cira!" I shouted her name. She jumped slightly but turned to look at me. "You will tell me what is going on and you will tell me now or I swear the first chance I get I'm taking Kai, and you will never see me again."

She chewed on her lip slightly, contemplating what to tell me and how much before she sighed, I guess she realized there was no point in hiding anything else from me.

"Years ago, I was supposed to marry Laurel." Shock wasn't the word I would use right now; it was more like disgusted. Not at my sister but at Ezra and Laurel. They couldn't get the oldest daughter to marry the creep, so they moved on to the naïve youngest daughter.

"He was the one I was betrothed to when I fell in love with Aris. It wasn't until after we were exiled that I figured out what their plan was."

"Plan? What plan? It can't be more power that Ezra wants, he's already the most powerful immortal in centuries."

Cira shook her head. "He's the most powerful *now*."

"What does that mean Cira, there is something you are not telling me, and I want to know what it is."

Cira sighed, "Have you not heard the whispers around the castle after all these years I've been away?" I had no idea what whispers she expected me to hear so I shook my head no and waited for her to continue. "Long ago, there was a prophecy foretold about this family. One that said we would be the end of it."

Chapter 20

For years I had done everything that I could to protect those that I care about. First it was my precious little willow, and over the last hundred years, it had also been my one true love. I tried to keep them both from seeing how bad the situation truly was, but for Aris, it didn't take much for him to see what was going on. He was the center of it after all. My little willow though, she had lasted much longer in the dark. Right under Ezra's thumb, having to do his bidding all alone in this castle after all these years. Being brainwashed into thinking he was a loving father who wanted nothing more than to protect his family. I wonder what kind of lie he's been telling her all these years to explain my absence.

My little willow has grown up now. That had happened while I had been forced away from her. She wasn't a child anymore and I wanted nothing more than to protect her even if that meant finally telling her the truth. She wanted to be treated as an adult and that's exactly what I would do for her.

"Ezra has overseen this land for as long as anyone can remember. There was even a story that once he went by another name, but that name was lost by time."

I grabbed Niyla's arm and pulled her over so we could both sit on the edge of the bed. She didn't take her eyes off me, and I could tell she was hanging on my every word. That's good that meant she was paying close attention and that's exactly what I wanted. She needed to be fully prepared for everything that was coming, which meant she needed to listen to every detail that I had to tell her.

"The details of his origin aren't even known, but around the time he came into power, he kept a witch as his main advisor."

"That isn't possible. There are no witches allowed on this island." Niyla said, interrupting me. Another lie he told.

"Not true, there is one. She lives further into the woods, in seclusion. The only one to know her whereabouts is Ezra himself. Mother doesn't even know." Her face twisted into that of confusion. There was a time years ago when our father had banned others from our island, only allowing our kind and a few select humans to be our slaves. No one knew why, but I found out the truth years ago.

"How can she advise him if she doesn't reside in the castle by his side with all the other aids he's had over the years?"

"Ezra has made all of us follow the ideology that we are the most powerful and because of that we should rule over every other race. When the others thought he was a dictator and chose not to follow what he wanted, rightly so, he had them either removed from the island or destroyed for their treason."

"Others? What others? None of this is making any sense Cira, why didn't I know anything about this?" Everything I was telling her was completely true but also a lot to take in. For a moment, I contemplated not telling her more. Maybe waiting until she has had time to process what I had told her so far, but against my better judgement, I figured it was better to treat it like a band aid and rip it off all at once.

"Immortals, witches, and humans are not the only species to walk this planet. There are many others that originated from this island. Some are barely surviving, being cut off from their motherland. Ezra knew this which is why he knew that for some being banished from here was worse than death."

Her eyes grew wide, but she didn't interrupt me this time. It must finally be sinking in the type of person our father was. To what extent he would go to just to keep himself in power. Being the cause of wiping out several other races wasn't the end of Ezra's cruelty. What I had to tell her would put the final nail in the coffin of how she views him from now until the day we finally destroyed him.

"This aid, prophesized, that there would be someone who would be a warrior strong enough to end his rule and take the mantle for themselves."

Niyla pulled her hands away, nervously rubbing them on her jean clad thighs. "I don't understand. Who is this warrior and what does it have to do with us?"

I was hoping she would ask that, because I wondered the same thing when I first heard the prophecy, that is until I found out the rest of it.

My mind was completely scrambled. I was having such a hard time following the things Cira was saying. There was so much I never knew about the place I grew up and even more I didn't know about the man who raised me. Ezra had always had a cruel side, I've known that my entire life, but every time I think I finally had him figured out. I finally knew the extent of his monstrous nature; I would learn something new about him that would turn me completely on my side.

This prophecy she was talking about seemed to be the key to understanding everything that had happened since the day she left me, and I wanted to know everything about it, especially if it had anything to do with Kai.

"This warrior," She started. "Would be of Ezra's blood and would be a hybrid."

"A hybrid?"

"Yes, a hybrid, but not just any hybrid. A hybrid born of human and vampire." I couldn't help but gasp a little. So that's what it was. Ezra didn't want Cira and I to mate with humans because he was afraid that any children we had would be his downfall. I came to a horrible realization in that moment, but I was almost afraid to say it out loud.

"But that means he knew that you were pregnant when he locked you away. It was intentional." I couldn't look her in the eyes, so I settled for staring at the top of her head. Nevertheless, I saw her nod her head yes.

When I went to speak with Ezra, he wouldn't outright admit it, maybe because he didn't want to tell me the truth about all of this, but I didn't need him to admit anything now. If he didn't know, it would be one hell of a coincidence and Ezra didn't do coincidences. This only proved that everything he did, he did with a purpose and now I knew what that purpose was.

One thing still didn't make sense to me though. "How does Laurel fit into all of this? Why is Ezra so insistent that he be the one we mate with?"

"There is a second part to the prophecy that says a warrior born of Ezra's blood and that of a witch would give him the power to conquer the world."

"A witch?"

Cira grabbed my chin and adjusted my face, so I had no choice but to look her in the eyes. "He didn't tell that either then?" she asked. I didn't respond I just stared at her in confusion and shock that after everything she just told me, there was still more that I was missing. "Laurel isn't a normal immortal. He's a hybrid, born of a witch and an immortal."

I got to my feet so fast, I stumbled slightly but caught myself. "You're not telling me what I think you're telling me are you?"

"Yes, Laurel is the product of an affair Ezra had with the witch. He is our brother."

"But that's impossible! Why would he keep that from us?"

"Ezra loves his secrets. Haven't you noticed how much stronger he is than we are. When Ezra mated with the witch, he thought that he would finally fulfill the prophecy and take over the world, but the prophecy calls for a daughter not a son."

This was all too much to take in. This room suddenly felt like a quarter of its normal size. The air was suddenly so stifling, and it felt like I couldn't breathe. Before Cira could stop me, I turned on my heels and ran to the door. I could hear Cira calling after me but that didn't slow me down. I yanked opened the door and ran face first into a solid chest. The impact caused me to land right on my ass. I looked up and saw the disgustingly annoying face of Laurel.

"Just the person I was looking for. It seems like fate that you would run into me like that doesn't it." He stretched out his hand for me to grab but I swatted it away. It would be a cold day in hell before I accept any kind of help from him.

"Oh, such a shame, I thought we were past all the hostility to-wards each other, we'll be family soon after all." His comment made me sick to my stomach. We were already family, and our father expected his two children, siblings, to marry each other just so he could take over the rest of the world. Laurel was not unaware of our relationship with each other and yet he was still going along with it.is

My face scrunched up in disgust. "Don't give me that look, I have a present for you."

"I don't want anything from you."

"I doubt that. I think you would enjoy this present very much." He held out a small folded up slip of paper.

I stared at it but didn't reach for it. "What is it?"

"It's the location of that pathetic human you let follow you around." In the blink of an eye, I snatched the paper from his fingers before he had a chance to change his mind.

Unfolding the paper, I read what was on it. Coordinates to a spot far in the woods, much further beyond where I've ever been. I guess it was foolish of me to think they might be holding him somewhere in the castle. "How do I know this is real and not some sort of trick?"

"Well, wouldn't you hate yourself if you didn't try to find out." He smirked at me, and I couldn't help but grind my teeth together. I hated him. I hated him and Ezra.

He was toying with me, I was certain, but he was right I wouldn't be able to live with myself if I had the opportunity to see Kai and I didn't take it.

"Is Aris with him?" Cira asked. We both turned to face her. For a second I forgot she was even in the room, my mind so consumed with thoughts of seeing Kai again.

Laurel chuckled before answering. "Of course not. Your human mate was killed back at your tiny little encampment. Did no one tell you that?"

A painful shriek was Cira's response as she crumbled to the ground, burying her face in her hands. I turned to face him, nothing but rage clouded my mind. Before I had a chance to think about what I was doing I pulled my leg back and kicked out with as much force as I could, landing a hit right in the middle of his abdomen. I heard a loud crack followed by Laurel flying back and crashing hard into the wall. He slid down to the floor, a few pieces of the crumbling wall falling on top of him.

I rushed to Cira's side, scooping her in my arms and holding her close. "You're a sick bastard!" I shouted at him. Laurel burst into a fit of laughter as he got to his feet and brushed off his black slacks, knocking as much of the white drywall from his pants as he could.

"That almost hurt. What is it that she calls you?" He turned his head up to the ceiling as if he was thinking and shoved his hands into his pockets. "Ah yes, try harder next time little willow." Rage shot through me at hearing him call me that. He was mocking my sister's pain. I shifted to get to my feet, but Cira grabbed my arm, pulling me back to her.

When I looked at her red, tear-stained face, I knew there was just no way I could leave her right now, so instead I watched as Laurel gave both of us one more gleeful smile and before leaving the room.

That son of a bitch, I would make him pay.

Chapter 21

A few hours had gone by since Laurel had told Cira that her mate was gone. She had been crying nonstop since. I suppose it is possible to eventually run out of tears because now she walked next to me in an incredibly dense part of the forest, well past the castle grounds, in complete silence. Ezra led the way and Laurel followed closely while Cira and I were left to trail behind. I noticed Cira's shoulders shaking slightly as she tried to refrain from making any noise. I knew it was a pride thing, she couldn't form anymore tears, but if she could, she would never want Ezra to see them.

Every so often I would see Laurel leaning into Ezra to whisper something, but I didn't even bother to try and listen in. As secretive as the two of them had been this entire time, it wouldn't have even surprised me if they chose to speak in code just so I wouldn't know what they were talking about.

It wouldn't matter if I could understand them, as of now, I hadn't quite figured out a way to get rid of them both and currently Cira was not in the right head space to bounce ideas off. That essentially left me all alone to figure it out.

We walked for almost the entire night; the sun had set hours ago. I wasn't quite sure why wherever we were going, couldn't wait until morning, but I knew when we stopped walking, I would be with Kai, so I didn't complain. The forest grew increasingly dense the further we walked until it was almost impossible to get through. We couldn't see anything in front of us besides trees and more trees. Add complete darkness to it, and I wasn't entirely sure how they were managing to navigate. Nevertheless, it didn't seem like we were lost, so I continued to follow along.

"We're here." Ezra announced. I looked around trying to figure out where here was, but all I could see was a wall of trees.

"There's nothing here."

Laurel turned to smile at me before stepping toward a patch of trees. He waved his hands at them and right before my eyes the trees shimmered and disappeared. Left standing in their place was a small rundown shack. The walls were clearly made of wood, cracked, and falling apart. The roof oddly enough looked like it was made from only hay. One tiny window and a door that looked like it could barely stand a strong gust of wind.

It looked uninhabitable. There was a witch living here? It didn't look like anyone had lived here in years. Laurel stepped toward the shack and opened the door. Inside, you could only see darkness and nothing else. He stepped inside without looking back, Ezra following close behind. I exchanged a cautious look with Cira before I followed them in.

The moment I stepped through the door, it was like I stepped into a completely different building. Darkness no longer surrounded us, instead bright red walls stood on all four sides of us. The room was larger on the inside than it appeared on the outside. Instead of a single drab room, on one side sat a small open kitchen and on the other was a small living space with a little couch and even a bookcase full of old dusty books. Ahead of us there was a hallway that led to a few other rooms, probably a bedroom.

This entire place was completely created by the witch's power, but something told me this wasn't even close to the extent of her abilities. How has she gone unnoticed this entire time? This much power, I should've heard something about her after all these years even if it was only whispers.

Ezra walked over to the couch and sat down, crossing his legs, and getting comfortable as if being here was something he did regularly. How many times has he come out here behind my mother's back. Did she know about the affair? About Laurel?

About the witch? Or was she just a pawn to him like the rest of us.

"Well, what do we have here?" My head shot up at the voice. A voice I'm used to hearing spoken a lot softer, one I hadn't heard since the night I escaped that stupid birthday party. That bright red hair, and those dark brown eyes.

Harper. My most loyal servant. I trusted her with all my secrets and, for years, I had considered her an older sister. Now, here she stood in the middle of the secret shack that I never knew about on the outskirts of the castle grounds. Why?

"It's been a while, Niyla." She smiled at me sweetly before she bowed. "Oh, I'm sorry where are my manners, I mean your grace."

My mouth hung open for a second and it seemed like I couldn't form a coherent thought. I was so confused, and I had no idea what was going. It sounded like Harper and for the most part it looked like Harper, but something was different. She almost looked younger than I remember. Her skin looked smooth; her eyes looked brighter.

"What the hell is going?" Frustration was running through me. Me being lied to by everyone was clearly the default setting.

"Oh sweetheart, you didn't tell her?" she turned to face Laurel. Walking over to him, she reached up and gently caressed his cheek.

"Sorry mother, my fiancée and I haven't had a lot of time alone to discuss the in-laws."

Mother? There's no way she could be his mother, she was immortal and he was only half. Cira grabbed my arm and pulled me back. She leaned close before she whispered to me. "She's the witch Niyla." I couldn't help the little gasp that escaped from me. That couldn't be true. I would've known, or she would've told me, right?

When I looked back at Harper, she was staring at me with a sadistic smile, almost like she couldn't be happier that I was in this situation. This wasn't the same sweet smile I was used to her giving me over the years. The more I looked at her, the more it seemed unbelievable that this was the same person.

"Niyla dear, you don't look happy to see me." She stood in front of Cira and me. With her this close, I could feel something was not normal about her. It was almost like an aura that surrounded her, it felt... dangerous. "Oh, and look it's Cira too, I wasn't sure I would get to see you again."

Since Cira was still holding onto me, I felt the exact moment her body stiffened. I turned my head to look at her and I could see the confusion written on her face.

"You know me?" she asked.

"Of course, don't you remember? Maybe this will help." Harper lifted her arm and snapped her finger. Suddenly Harper wasn't standing in front of us anymore, instead there stood a woman a few inches taller than Harper had been. She had caramel skin and tight ringlets all over her head.

"Mia?"

"Yes, my sweet. Now you remember."

Harper or Mia or whatever her name was turned her back to us and made her way over to Ezra. She sits down next to him and places her hand on his thigh.

"Oh my god, it was you, wasn't it?" Cira shouted. She let go of my arm and stepped in front of me. Her face was twisted up in anger. Her fangs were fully extended, and her eyes were dark red. If her hands weren't balled into fists, I'm sure I would see her claws fully extended too.

"You are the one who found out about Aris and me. You turned us in."

The witch covered her mouth and giggled but didn't give Cira a clear answer. All the pieces started falling into place. The night I left, the only person who knew where I was going, the only one who helped me get away was Harper. She is how they knew I made it off the island, the reason why they chose to check the docks. She was also probably how that guard found us at one of the ports we docked at.

I wasn't sure how she found out about Kai but with her level of power I'm sure it wouldn't be difficult for her to spy on everything I was doing while remaining on this island. Was she really the one to put Kai's life in danger? Was he being held captive having who knows what done to him while I'm being forced to marry my own brother, was that all because of her?

I don't know what came over me, it was like I had left my own body, and I was watching everything happen from the sidelines. One second, I was standing behind Cira listening to everything and coming to the realization that everything that had happened over these last couple weeks, years were all planned by these two power hungry psychos and the next I was standing in front Harper, straddling her hips on the couch, my hand around her throat.

I dug my claws into the sides of her neck, squeezing as hard as I could and watching in satisfaction as the dark red blood leaked from the gaping holes I was creating. I wanted to rip her throat out and see if she could still run her mouth without it. I squeezed and tugged but before I had a chance to rip her throat out, I was hit with a blast of energy so strong it pushed me back, slamming me into Cira and then throwing us both into the stainless-steel refrigerator. I screamed out when all my exposed skin encountered the refrigerator. It wasn't made from steel, it was silver.

I looked at Harper, but she hadn't even moved. Was this the strength of her ability. How the hell was I supposed to kill her if I couldn't even get close enough to do anything.

"Ezra darling, I thought after all these years, you would've taught your daughters some manners. Attacking someone in their own home, I guess spending time with those humans have turned them into savages." I grit my teeth, the pain in my wrists and the back of my neck from touching the silver becoming unbearable. The way we were thrown into the refrigerator made it so Cira was in front of me, pressing me harder into it, but at least that meant she wasn't in contact with it as well.

"Let us go!" she shouted out. Harper put her finger to her chin, looking up at the ceiling as if she had to think about it.

"I'll let you down if you two behave. No more trying to kill me, it's futile anyway." I hesitated but we both shook our heads yes. My hands were becoming numb, and I wasn't sure how much more abuse they could take.

That strong force we felt moments ago suddenly disappeared and Cira and I landed hard on the wood floor, me on top of her.

"Now then, we have much to discuss. First things first, I would love to plan a big wedding, doesn't that sound wonderful?" Her constant switch in mood was off-putting. I couldn't seem to gauge what she would do next which also wouldn't help in the killing her part of whatever plan I managed to come up with. She went on and on about different ideas she had for the wedding. Things like what kind of dress I should wear, how I should style my hair. She even went as far as to try and discuss what pieces of lingerie I should wear during my wedding night.

She sounded just like any normal mother of the groom except she wasn't, and this wasn't the time to feed this strange delusion she was concocting.

"I want to see Kai, now!" I interrupted her rambling. She huffed and folded her arms across her chest.

"Rude, but very well." Harper snapped her fingers, and a glass wall appeared in front of me. "Take a look." She spoke.

I stepped forward and peered into the glass. At first, I only saw myself but then the image wavered, and I could see Kai and his beautiful blonde hair. He sat in the corner of a dark room. His knees up to his chest and his head leaned down into them. I couldn't tell where he was, but I was sure he wasn't back at the castle. This cell looked nothing like the one we were held in.

"Take me to him. You promised I could see him." I couldn't take my eyes off the scene in front of me out of fear that if I looked away for even a second, he would disappear, and I would never see him again.

"We said you could see him, taking you to him was not part of the arrangement."

I reached out and tried to touch the image but just as quickly as it was there, it disappeared. My heart skipped a beat, and I turned back to them. I could feel myself becoming desperate, but I was trying my hardest not to show them. It seemed like everyone in this room had an upper hand over me and I didn't like it, nor did I know how to change it.

"Let him go, he has nothing to do with this."

"See daughter, that's where you're wrong." Ezra got to his feet and approached Cira and me. "Both of you disobeyed our most sacred rule, you cannot mark a human." His eyes darted back and forth between the two of us, making sure he looked us both in the eyes. He was enjoying this immensely; he knew looking at us right in the eyes would tell him just how much we were suffering, and he enjoyed every part of it. These were the traits of someone who cared about nothing but himself and what he wanted.

Ezra walked over to Laurel and placed his hand on his shoulder. "This was to be the person you mated with, but because you thought it wise to do whatever you wanted to do without considering the consequences, these are the results. Now your precious little humans have everything to do with this."

"We've already marked them, there's no changing that, so what do you want from us? You've already killed Aris and if you kill Kai, we have no reason to do anything you want." I pushed back my shoulders and tried to look stronger and braver than I felt at this moment.

Ezra let out a roaring laugh. "Is that what he told you, that we had already killed your sister's human mate?" He slapped Laurel on the back again, Laurel standing there smirking.

Cira took a step forward. "So, he's alive?" she asked.

Ezra shrugged. "For now. As long as it's been since you've marked him, you would know if he had really been killed."

"Not true darling," Harper spoke up. "That was my doing, just a little trick Laurel and I decided to play on her. I was curious to see how she would react. Plus call it motherly payback for her rejecting my son all those years ago."

Ezra smiled and gave a slight shrug. Cira's knees buckled and I barely managed to catch her before she crumbled. A relieved look on her face. They were all sadistic, she told a lie like this because her disgusting son had his feelings hurt.

"It also isn't true that there is nothing we can do about those pesky marks you see." Harper stretched her arms above her head and yawned, like the conversation itself was boring to her. "I can remove the mark from that human so that you can mark another."

I could feel my eyes grow wide as I stared at her. That couldn't be true. Even if she was the most powerful witch in the world, there was no way she would be able to take that mark off the side of his neck.

"You're face tells me you're skeptical of my power. If I was able to tamper with the connection of two mates, that should show you what I'm capable of."

"You expect me to believe you can remove a mark that's supposed to last until death? What do you plan to do, kill him? I already told you if you do you won't get anything from me."

"You don't have to believe it. All you must do is what you're told."

I helped Cira back to her feet before staring Harper down. "And what is that exactly?"

"All you must do is convince that innocent little human that you no longer love him. You better make it good, or I'll gut your sister and her mate like the abominations they are."

Chapter 22

This was crazy, they were crazy, and I would be stupid to believe anything either one of them said. I wasn't sure how this plan of theirs was supposed to work, all I know is that the first half of it was already impossible to do.

They wanted me to convince Kai that I didn't want to be with him anymore. How did they hope I could accomplish something like that? He was marked which meant I would love and want to be with him forever, there was no way to change that, and that's exactly what I voiced.

"That's not possible, he would know I was lying. The mark would tell him so.

"A mere human who knows nothing of our kind nor how to interpret the things they feel from the mark. With how recently you marked him, some of the abilities have not fully been developed yet, which means, he would never be able to tell if you're lying or not if you make it believable." Harper said, flicking her wrist to dismiss my words. "Do whatever you have to, to make it happen."

Harper snapped her finger again and the image of Kai reappeared in the mirror.

"Go ahead, see your human lover one final time, and tell him what you must. Just make it good or I'll rip your sister to shreds and trust me, I'll make it hurt." To emphasize her point, she lifted her arm and waved her wrist. Suddenly, Cira dropped to the ground and began screaming. I watched in horror as several dark red spots began forming on the sleeves of her shirt. The blood dripped down her arms and off her fingertips causing large pools of blood to form around her.

Tears formed in her eyes and raced down her cheeks as she stared at me begging me to make her stop.

"Stop!" I shouted. "I'll do it, just leave her alone." Instantly Cira stopped screaming. The blood that had pooled around her and the blood staining her clothes both disappeared.

"I'm glad you saw it my way. Now off you go." Harper motioned toward the mirror. I reached out my hand to tentatively touch the smooth surface, but the moment I did, my fingers passed right through. I yanked my hand back when I felt a cold breeze touch my fingertips.

I took a deep breath and pulled back my shoulders before approaching the mirror. I gave one final look over my shoulder at Cira. She stared at me with concern written all over her face, so I smiled back at her in my best attempt at being reassuring. I didn't need her to worry anymore then she already was. I would handle everything.

Turning back to the mirror, I stepped through it. My shoes made a crunching sound when they landed on the stone covered ground. It was dark, pitch black. If it wasn't for my superior sight as an immortal, I don't even think I would be able to see my hand in front of my own face.

Looking around, I attempted to take in as much of my surroundings as I could. There wasn't much to see, it looked like I was in a cave, but I had no idea where. There were rock-covered walls all around me and an opening on each side. I was hoping to see a light coming from one of the directions, at least that would help me indicate which way was the exit in case I found an opportunity to grab Kai and escape. It didn't matter though; I wouldn't be able to do anything without putting Aris and Cira in danger.

For now, until it was safe, the best course of action would be to follow the witches demands which were, break Kai's heart and make it believable.

I grit my teeth to keep them from chattering. It was so cold here I could see the smoke coming from my nose every time I exhaled. I tried balling myself up as much as I could, hoping to keep myself warm. It wasn't working, nothing I seemed to do was. Blowing on my hands, rubbing my arms, nothing.

I had no idea where I was or where Niyla was. When I had woken up to screaming and realized I was alone in bed, I thought the scream had come from Niyla.

The truth wasn't any better than what I thought. Seeing those men dressed in all black rushing in, staking every vampire in their path watching small children literally denigrate right before your eyes did something to a person.

Through all that horror I had to watch, all I could think about was where was Niyla? I wondered if those men had already gotten to her, driving a stake through her chest but then I thought, there had to be a reason we were left alive in that cell instead of immediately killed when that son of a bitch found us in Milo's home.

Knowing that there was a good chance Niyla had made it out of the whole ordeal unscathed was the only thing that had kept me going. I had to stay alive and keep my mind sharp so the first chance I got I could escape and find her.

I shifted, squeezing my knees closer to my chest. My chains rattled and I wondered how long they would leave me here until

I eventually froze to death, or was this also in some way part of her father's plan?

What could his plan be though? To still try and marry her off to that scruffy haired bastard who managed to track her down? But that didn't make much sense considering that we were already bonded. Niyla had told me there was no way to remove the mark and according to Aris, Niyla couldn't drink any other blood besides mine, so what did her father hope to accomplish with all of this?

Why had I been separated from the others? At the very least, Aris should've been captured with me, right? I saw them grab him, but I didn't see what happened after that.

My thoughts were interrupted by a scraping sound coming from the darkness. I didn't know what it was because honestly, it was just an assumption that I was in this cave by myself.

I braced myself as the scraping sound seemed like it was getting closer. I pressed myself further into the wall behind me, trying but failing to make myself as invisible as I could. It could be another vampire or some other kind of creature that liked to call these caves home, I had no idea, but whatever it was, I sure hope it didn't like meat.

Finally, the scraping stopped and instead I heard a soft whisper. "Kai?" I breathed a sigh of relief and struggled to get to my feet. I could only move so far because of the chains, so instead I waited for Niyla to come closer and loosen the chains.

Surprisingly she didn't move, she just stood there staring at me with this unreadable expression on her face.

"Niyla, I was worried about you. I thought your father had taken you again." Still no response.

"Did they hurt you?" I asked. She still didn't respond, instead, she took a few more steps toward me. The darkness surrounding us didn't provide great lighting, but at least this close, I could get a better look at her face. It was completely blank. I couldn't read her at all. "I wasn't sure if you were hurt or not."

"That's not your concern, I'm fine." I couldn't help the slight flinch at the tone in her voice. Why did she sound so cold, almost like I was a stranger or something.

"Why wouldn't it be my concern?" I raised an eye brown in confusion and attempted to take a step towards her, but I felt the immediate resistance of the chain. They didn't provide any slack unlike the chains of my previous prison.

"I think your energy would be much better spent worrying about yourself." I felt a chill race down my spine. I felt an almost suffocating sense of dread overtake me. Something was seriously wrong here. She told me that because of the mark, I should be able to tell what was going on in her head, but I couldn't feel anything. It didn't feel like the mark was there at all.

"What's going on Niyla? We don't have time for this; we need to get out of here?"

For the first time since she stepped foot in this cave, she gave me a little smile. I felt the puff of air trapped in my chest release slightly but not completely, I had the feeling something still wasn't right.

Niyla took another step towards me and placed her hand on my chest. Instantly the spot she touched warmed. I barely felt the cold anymore.

Smiling at me sweetly, she asked, "What makes you think you're getting out of here?" Her smile disappeared and she took a step back from me. H

"You're a foolish human to believe anything that has ever happened between us was real, you were just necessary for me to get what I want. Now that I have, you're not needed anymore."

I stared at her not sure what to say. I didn't understand what she was talking about. Instead of questioning her any further, I opted to just let her talk and hope at some point I would catch on to what's happening right now.

I stood and waited for her to say more, but she didn't and since I hadn't said anything in response, she took that as her queue to leave. She turned and began walking off.

"Wait" I called after her, attempting again to move closer to her forgetting about the chains until I felt the painful tug on my wrists.

She stopped but didn't turn around. "What's going on, what do you mean by your *plan*?"

There was a period of silence where nothing could be heard besides our breathing and the faint sound of water droplets hitting a puddle of water in the distance. That moment seemed to stretch on for so long that I almost thought for a second she wasn't going to say anything at all.

That is until she broke out into a fit of laughter before turning back to face me. "Just what I said." She reached up and tugged at the hair tie keeping her ponytail in place, causing it to come lose and her hair to tumble down her back.

Niyla ran her fingers through her now lose curls giving her scalp a little massage. She breathed a sigh of relief and dropped her arms to her side.

"It feels so good to finally be done with this." She closed her eyes and smiled, a look of pure relief on her face.

"Niyla, tell me what's going on. You're not making any sense." The frustration was setting in. I had been stuck in this cave worried about her for I don't know how long. Cold, alone, starving and the first time I see her, she's acting like she doesn't want to get these chains off so we can get out of here and as far away from her psycho family as we could as fast as we could.

I deserved an explanation of what's going on and why she's behaving the way she is because frankly there have been a lot of things that she has been conveniently forgetting to explain.

Niyla groaned and rolled her eyes. "Humans can be so dense sometimes. Do I have to really spell it out for you?"

"I don't want to be with you. I used you because I was trying to find my sister and now that I have, I don't need you anymore."

Her words would've stung more if they made sense, but they didn't. "How does marking me help you find your sister; you had no idea she was even alive until I put the thought in your head."

She sighed. "How irritating, I knew my sister was alive all along. I needed a reason bad enough for my father to lock me away. Something so bad that it could lead to my father trying to kill me. That was the only way to draw my sister out of hiding."

I swallowed the lump that began forming in my throat. That couldn't be true. "You're lying. I saw the look on your face when I suggested it, you had no idea if she was alive or not."

Niyla covered her mouth to try to hide her smirk, but she couldn't hide the chipper tone in her voice. "All a testament to my acting abilities. Pretty excellent, right? I had you completely fooled."

She lied to me, about everything. She took the role damsel in distress to new heights, making me think that marking me was an accident. That she had no idea about what happened to her sister. Even going as far as pretending to be shocked at the news of what happened to Cira all those years ago. All of it was a lie and I fell for all of it. Whatever happened from now on was completely my own fault.

"Well, if we're done here, I really should get back. I have a wedding to plan."

My heart skipped a beat. She was planning to marry Laurel. After everything that had happened, she was planning to marry him anyway?

"So, you're just going to leave me here?"

She shrugged, turning to leave. "Someone will come to let you go after the wedding. Have a nice life human." She waved her hand over her shoulder and disappeared into the dark. Now I know the truth, something I should've recognized from the very beginning when she wouldn't tell me the truth about why she stowed away on my ship, Niyla and her entire species were nothing but liars.

My reflection stared back at me unblinkingly in the glass mirror that sat in front of me. My knees ached from kneeling on the hard floors for so long, but I wasn't sure what to expect if I tried to move. The witched hadn't done more than wave her hand and my skin literally melted from my bones. I didn't know what she would do if I moved before Niyla had returned from wherever that mirror led.

I couldn't help but wonder what Ezra and the witch had planned. Yes, it was obvious that they still hoped to marry one of us off to Laurel so that Ezra could get his super soldier, but we had both already marked someone, there was no way to change that. I wasn't even sure it was possible for either one of us to be able to procreate with Laurel if our marks were on Aris and Kai.

They had this made-up story about the witch having the ability to remove the mark. She was powerful alright, but could it really be true that she would be able to do something like that. If she was and she managed to remove Kai's mark what was to stop her from doing the same to Aris too or was that her plan all along, that way if one of us stepped out of line she could kill us, and she would still have another daughter to carry out her plan. There had to be a reason she kept us both alive besides leverage to get Niyla to do what she wanted.

If that was the only reason, there would be nothing keeping us alive if their plan worked and she was able to marry Niyla off to Laurel. Besides, I couldn't let my sister sacrifice her life for my sake even if it turned out to be the only way to get Aris back, there had to be another way.

I took my eyes off the mirror and instead focused on looking around the room for something, anything that could help me get the upper hand over the three of them. I had to come up with a plan of escape before Niyla returned, which meant I had to think fast.

There wasn't much around, just the bare necessities to make it a livable home. A small couch, a tiny coffee table. The kitchenette only had a fridge and a couple counters, strangely no stove, did the witch not eat? Or maybe she just took all her meals back at the castle, but then why a fridge.

"How much longer must we wait mother; this is becoming tedious." Laurel had been pacing back and forth behind me, huffing and puffing ever since Niyla went through that glass. It was strange that he was so anxious, especially considering how relaxed Ezra and the witch seemed to be in this moment. They were under the impression their entire plan was going to see fruition, but something was making Laurel not so sure, I wonder if there was a way to exploit that insecurity.

"Relax dear, let the girl have her final moments with the human. It makes no difference to us." The witch was sitting close to Ezra. Their thighs touched and she was looking deep into his eyes, so close, it looked like they were seconds away from kissing. It was disgusting to watch really; did he love my mother at all or was that one of his little mind games too. It was honestly hard to tell with him anymore.

This was my opportunity though; how far could I push this? "I wouldn't be too sure about that." I kept my eyes on Laurel's legs as he paced back and forth. I tried my hardest to hide the satisfied smirk I had when he stopped walking to face me. All his attention now on me.

"What does that mean?" He asked.

"You sent my sister back to the man she marked. Who's to say they aren't making a baby right now, that would sure ruin your plans, wouldn't it?" I had no idea where I was going with this, nor what the outcome would be but maybe an idea will arise if I provoke them enough.

I looked up just long enough to see that stoic mask slip from Laurel's face for just a second before he quickly put it back. Was that concern I saw? Maybe doubt.

"Nice try little Cira." The witch chimed in before Laurel had a chance to say anything. "Your sister would never do something like that especially with your life in my hands. That seems more like something you would do."

I flinched at the little dig because she wasn't wrong. That's essentially what I had done to Niyla all those years ago. I chose my happiness over her safety, leaving her in the hands of our psycho parents. None of this would be happening right now if I hadn't left her behind to leave with Aris. I should've taken her with me.

"Ah, did I strike a nerve." The witch got to her feet, making her way over to me. She crouched down and got close to my face. I could see my own reflection in her eyes. "You think you're smart, but you aren't."

"Smart enough to be with a man that only wants me." I said referring to Ezra. I guess that was all it took because the witch reached up and grabbed me by my hair, yanking it until I got to my feet. I screamed and grabbed her wrist, trying to prevent her from tugging any harder.

I pulled her arm trying to get her to let go but she didn't budge. At that moment, Niyla stepped back through the portal. She looked stunned, unsure of what move to make. I was distracted trying to get the witch to let me go, but Niyla disappeared from my view. She reappeared to my left, grabbing the witch by the back of the neck. She released her grip on me and turned around just in time to see Niyla shove a pin through her eye.

I reached up and touched my hair and realized my hair had come undone when the witch grabbed me by it. One of the pins I kept in my hair must've fallen out.

The witch screamed, grabbing for Niyla's hand. "Run Cira, find them!" She shouted at me, never taking her eyes off the witch. She put more force into the stab, fighting against the witch's strength.

In the corner of my eye, I could see Laurel and Ezra rushing towards me. I had to decide, stay and help my sister fight them off or do what she told me and run. There was a slim chance I would be able to help her at this moment so as much as it pained me, I did what she asked and what I had done all those years ago, I ran.

Chapter 23

I heard a loud crunch when my shoulder slammed into the wooden dresser. It splintered and I was just barely lucky enough not to get stabbed by one of the wooden slivers. I looked up in time to see the guard turn his nose up at me and close the door behind him.

I sighed and cradled my shoulder. It was broken, but I guess I should've expected something like this after what I had done. It shocked me really; I was able to make contact with the witch. It was a long shot, and I was almost positive if I tried anything, she would've killed us both. Whatever Cira said must've really upset her.

Cira. I hope she was able to get away. Ezra and Laurel were so distracted trying to separate me from the witch, Cira was able to slip out, now I had no idea where she was.

With any luck she would find Aris and Kai and get them as far away from this place as she possibly could.

The chances of her finding Kai were slim, I still wasn't sure where that place was. At least I could take satisfaction in the fact that she'll find Aris and get as far away from this place and Ezra as possible.

I might have to stay here and marry Laurel to satisfy my father to ensure Kai's safety but at least I would be the only one to suffer.

Ezra said tonight would be the night. No more stalling, no chances for anything else to go wrong. If what I said to Kai did its job, tonight the witch would perform some type of spell to make him mark free. Thanks to the full moon, she would have enough power to go through with it. Then there would be nothing to stop me from marking Laurel and doing what they wanted.

Struggling to get to my feet, I made my way to the large window on the other side of my bed. I looked out of the window and up at the sky. This island was so strange in many ways, one of them being that the nights seem to last much longer than the days. I never understood why that was, maybe it was magic. I never even noticed it until the first port we docked at on Kai's ship.

The sun seemed so bright and warm. I felt free, but that was all over now. I was back to being the poor little princess trapped in the tower, this time there would be no one to come and rescue me.

It was time, I could hear the guard who had been stationed outside my door banging or the bathroom door. The doorknob jiggled and he shouted for me to open the door and come out. It wasn't possible for me to do that right now; I was too busy holding my hair back as I leaned over the toilet throwing up everything I didn't eat today. Marrying Laurel was taking a real bad toll on me.

When I finally had it in my head that it was happening, it had quickly escalated from the thought making me sick to my stomach figuratively to it making me sick to my stomach physically.

A few servants had tried bringing me bottles or blood throughout the day, but I turned them all away. As long as my mark was still on Kai, I wouldn't be able to keep it down anyway, so there was no point in even trying.

At this rate, I was going to dry myself out before the ceremony and be nothing but a dried up, mummy like corps walking down the aisle. Then again maybe that wouldn't be such a bad thing. Unfortunately, though, I couldn't do anything but what they wanted if I wanted to make sure Kai stayed safe.

I guess the guard's impatience won in the end because a few seconds later, the door to the bathroom burst open and he walked in, completely filling the doorframe. I didn't like the way he looked at me, especially considering, I was confident I was stronger than he was.

It wouldn't be hard at all to make him show a little respect, but I had to keep it together. "Your father would like for you to meet him in the dining hall, it is time for the first part of the ceremony."

I sighed and got to my feet. I had been forced into wearing this stupid wedding dress the witch had insisted on. It was blood red with crystals framing the sweetheart neckline and making a path all the way down the center.

The extra poof at the bottom made it increasingly difficult to move around in, which in hindsight might've been part of their plan from the beginning. Less mobility means less likely to make a run for it.

I smoothed out any wrinkles that might've formed while sitting on the floor and followed the guard out of the bathroom. We maneuvered through the maze of my home until we made it to the dining area. There we found Ezra, Laurel, the witch, and a man I've never seen before. He was dressed in all black and strangely wore dark sunglasses. His hands were clasped in front of him, and he stood so still, if I didn't know any better, I would think he was a statue.

There was something off about him I could sense he wasn't a human, but he didn't seem to be immortal either. Was he another witch or maybe a hybrid? That could be why I couldn't determine what he was. When I first meant Laurel, I just assumed he was immortal but something about him did feel off.

"Ahh, it's the lovely bride to be." Ezra spread his arms wide, grabbing me and pulling me into a tight hug then kissed the top of my forehead. The number of times a day Ezra switches personalities is unending and extremely hard to keep up with.

He pulled back and brushed any lose hair over my shoulder, giving me a once over with his eyes to make sure I looked just right for the occasion. "You look just perfect honey." The witch said making sure she kept her distance. She had transformed herself back into the Harper I knew, bright red hair and soft brown eyes. Eyes that I use to be able to trust, but it wouldn't make any sort of difference, I could never look at her the same and I would never trust her again. I noticed the eyepatch the moment I stepped into the dining room, and I can't express how much joy it brought me to see her with it.

I couldn't tell because there was so much blood at the time, but I was pretty sure I had caused her to completely lose the eye. At the time I was mostly focused on the surprised fact that the witch could bleed. For some reason I had the impression that she couldn't.

"Enough with the niceties, let's get on with the spell shall we." Laurel has had an annoyed look on his face for a while now. I was starting to think that it was just his resting face. I understood what Ezra and the witch gained out of this whole arrangement but not what did Laurel gained. Afterall, the only part he had to play was mark me and assist in having a child. A child I'm sure Ezra would insist on raising in his own image, so what was Laurel's end goal?

"Oh, dear there's no need to be so impatient. This is your wedding day, try to enjoy it a little. I know I am." She smirked at me. I knew she was enjoying my misery, but I didn't have to make it easy for her.

"You know, seeing you with that eyepatch on really does make this a great day." Her smile dropped and even from this distance I could hear her grinding her teeth. Instead of responding like I hoped she would, she motioned for us to stand in the middle of the grand room.

I stood facing Laurel, my father stood behind me and the witch stood behind him. The strange man with the dark glasses stood in the middle of both of us.

He opened a book that he pulled out from under his arms. I hadn't even noticed it there. "I will read from the book of the ancestors before we begin the spell." The stranger began reading a few excerpts from the ancient book. I had no idea what he was saying, he spoke in a language I had never heard before.

I've been to a few weddings throughout the years, and I don't remember this being part of it. "What is he reading?" I asked.

Ezra shushed me so the man could finish and only after the man finished did the witch explain it to me. "It is the ancient language of the witches. I need to summon all the strength of those before me to complete the spell of the mark removal." Now it makes sense. I couldn't figure out what the stranger was because he was a witch, or at least part witch.

The witch took the strangers place in the center of us and held her hand out to me. "I need your blood." I held out my hand for her. She lifted the hem of her dress and pulled a dagger from a sheath on her thigh. She held my wrist with one hand and quickly sliced a huge gash right in the middle of my hand with the other. I flinched but the grip she had on my wrist prevented me from being able to pull away. She let the blood drip into a large golden chalice.

The moment the blood began to pool, it turned white. The witch mumbled a few words under her breath, waving her hand over the chalice. The lights in the huge chandelier over our heads flickered before completely going out, surrounding us in darkness.

A burst of light shot out from the chalice and disappeared over our head. I dropped my gaze back to the witch and realized, blood was dripping from her nose, and her entire body was practically vibrating.

Glancing at Laurel, I thought maybe he would show a little concern at how much power his mother was exerting, but his face remained the same way it had been, like everything about this situation was one big inconvenience to him.

The witch continued to mumble and suddenly the blood began to boil and smoke, like she was somehow heating it up. She began reciting her spell faster and louder, dropping to her knees but still clutching the chalice. Finally, she shouted one final word and turned her face up to the ceiling.

I watched in amazement as the blood turned from white to black and then back to white before ending back to blood red.

"What does that mean, is it done?" Laurel asked the question my mind was wondering.

The witch got to her feet and looked down at the chalice. She swirled the blood around a few times before bringing it to her lips. She took a gulp before cringing and spitting the blood out.

The witch tossed the chalice behind her, and it landed in the fireplace, causing the fire to roar to life. I could only take her reaction as a sign that it in fact did not.

She suddenly turned her furious gaze on me and before I had a chance to react, it felt like all the oxygen had been sucked right out of my lungs. I grabbed at my neck, trying my hardest to take a breath, but to no avail.

"You stupid bitch!" She shouted as she stalked toward me. Her walk was so menacing, if I wasn't struggling to breathe right now, it might've frightened me. "I gave you one job, to make the stupid human fall out of love with you and you couldn't even do that."

She raised her hand high, and I braced myself for impact. "You heartless bitch." I turned my head as much as I could towards the sound of the voice. Cira.

Chapter 24

"Well, look who it is, the disgusting brat who rejected my precious son." It appeared the witch's powers tightened their grip on my throat. I clawed at my neck trying my hardest to take a big gulp of air.

Cira scoffed and took a few tentative steps towards us. She held up her hands to show that she had nothing in them. "You're not still mad about that are you? That was years ago, I think it's time you both got over it." I saw how her body stiffen, and I could swear I saw a faint glow in her eyes. "Darling you've ruined our plans once before, you think I'm supposed to just forgive you for something like that?"

"Oh, I never said that." Cira gave a slight shrug and moved a little closer. "Frankly, I couldn't give a flying rat's ass about your forgiveness. I just want you to let go of my sister and get the hell out of my home."

I guess that amount of disrespect was enough to cause the witch to finally snap. She lunged for Cira. The witch's spell wore off and I slumped to the ground gasping for air.

Cira and the witch collided causing Cira to fly back into the wall right by the door she had just walked through. The witch didn't let up, she closed the distance between the two of them, putting her forearm under her throat putting just enough pressure there to cause her face to turn red but not enough to kill her.

I tried to catch my breath as quickly as possible so that I could help but as soon as I got to my feet Laurel stepped in my path. "Now, now sweetheart, you wouldn't want to interrupt their bonding time." He took a step towards me, grabbing me by my forearm and squeezing. I winced but didn't try to pull away.

"You and your whims set our plans back years and you think that you can just get away with it because you're a *Grey*." The witch spat the venom in Cira's face. I could see her putting more force into her arm, cutting off more of Cira's oxygen.

Cira swung her leg up and kicked out hard, kicking the witch in the stomach. She lost her grip and fell back releasing Cira.

"No" She struggled to get out. "Aris was never a whim and as far as that stupid name, if I never heard it again, I would be too ecstatic." Cira charged the witch again, lowering her body so she could aim right for her stomach.

The witch side stepped her, waving her hand and sending Cira through the glass mirror that sat above the fireplace. Cira screamed as she made impact and I tried again to pull away from Laurel but he tightened his grip even more and yanked me back towards him, backing us further away from the fight.

"Who cares about that stupid human anyway. He's nothing but a walking feed bag to you, that's all they all are. You could've ruled over them all right along with my son. We did you a favor by getting rid of that abomination growing in your womb. You should be thanking us."

With every word she said the rage began boiling inside of me. What she was saying to Cira, she might as well have been saying to me as well. I wanted to rip her fucking head off, but I was trying to keep my anger in check. We were outnumbered and all three of them were much more powerful than we were. I had to think of a way out of this.

Why would Cira come back. I told her to run and to come back without a plan, what was she thinking?

"Final warning witch. You're starting to piss me off, let my sister go or face the consequences."

The witch broke into a hearty laugh. "Right, and what do you thi-" That was all she was able to say before I watched Cira speed across the room and put her fist right through the witch's chest and pull back her heart.

The witch's eyes were wide as she stared at her in complete shock. A silent scream on her lips as her eyes rolled back. Icicles began forming on her body, starting from her feet, and quickly spreading all the way up her body until she was one huge ice statue. A statue that toppled over and smashed into a million tiny pieces.

The witch was dead.

I couldn't believe it; Cira had actually killed her.

I felt Laurel dig his claws into my arm. I turned to look up at his face and in the blink of an eye, he had pressed a silver blade to my throat. The rage was evident on his face. He pressed the blade to my throat causing the skin to sizzle.

I ground my teeth to keep from screaming out. Cira rushed toward us which made Laurel drag the blade across my neck, slicing through the skin and drawing blood. "Come any closer and I'll remove her head from her shoulders."

She hesitated but took another step towards us. "You're bluffing. You need her, you won't kill her."

He shook his head, slicing away at my neck again. "On the contrary, I only need one of you. I could kill your sister and still achieve what I want with you."

Laurel took another step back. "Which one will it be?" He asked. "Will it be you or your darling little sister that takes on the responsibility of being my wife?" He paused for a second, smirking, then he licked his lips and planted a kiss on my cheek.

"*All* the responsibilities of being my wife." I shivered involuntarily, a feeling of disgust running through my veins.

"Ah, it seems you're a little too eager to get started my darling." Laurel slipped his arm around waist, pulling me close, pressing my ass against his crotch. I tried jerking away from him again, but that only succeeded in making the wound on my neck even worse.

"You have five seconds to let my woman go before I drive a stake through your hand." My head jerked up at the sound of the voice. Kai stood in the doorway. His blonde locks looked soaked and stuck to his forehead. He was dressed in the clothes of our blood slaves, a plain white button up shirt, black bottoms with a red sash tied around his waist and a metal collar around his neck. Even his clothes were a dirty, wet mess. Kai looked out of breath and slightly flushed but the main thing I did notice was the huge stake in his hand.

Laurel sighed. "Who invited the disgusting human to our wedding. Honestly darling, I thought I told you not to mail out his invitation." He jerked my head back, exposing more of my neck and making sure Kai had a good view of the blood dripping from it.

"That wasn't a request, I said let her go." Kai moved towards us until he stood next to Cira.

"And if I don't, what can a pathetic little weak human like you do to me?" Laurel laughed.

Kai folded his arms across his chest and smiled. "Oh, I don't have to do anything isn't that right Niyla." Kai looked right at me, looking deep into my eyes and suddenly it was like something clicked in my head.

I hadn't realized, I could feel Kai again. Now that the witch is dead, whatever spell she cast to disrupt our link was gone. The smallest sliver of hope began to spread throughout my body. I needed to get out of Laurel's grip fast before he realized what had happened.

Taking a deep breath, I released the grip I had on Laurel's wrist, making sure to keep my head as still as possible so I wouldn't make the wound there any worse than it already was.

"Given up, have we?" Laurel asked. His mocking tone only succeeded in infuriating me even more. I couldn't wait to wipe that stupid grin off his face.

I pulled back my arm and swung hitting Laurel in his forearm. I doubted it would hurt him much; I just needed it to catch him off guard enough to shift the knife away from my throat.

Laurel grunted slightly and pulled back his arm a little, just enough to create enough space for me to sidestep, bring my leg forward and then back as hard as I could.

Lucky for me, my aim was spot on. I hit Laurel in that sweet spot right between his legs. He shouted out and released me, dropping to his knees and clutching himself. Thank those above, vampire or not that spot was just as vulnerable to any man.

In a flash I was standing next to Cira and Kai. Laurel quickly got to his feet, squaring his shoulders as if he was ready to charge all three of us.

All his attention was so focused on us, he didn't notice the shadow standing behind him, but I did.

Laurel took a step toward us, taking the shadow off the figure that stood behind him. It was Aris. I wasn't sure how he'd managed to get into the room without three immortals noticing but he did.

Being as quiet as he possibly could, Aris took a few steps forward before jumping on Laurel's back and tying a rope around his neck. One end of the rope was connected to the chandelier above, which provided Aris with the right amount of leverage to overpower him.

He pulled the rope as tight as he could as Laurel thrashed about trying to get Aris off his back. Cira took a step forward to help Aris, but Kai beat her to it.

Kai grabbed the other end of the rope, using the extra slack to tie it around Laurel's legs causing him to fall and the rope around his neck to tighten. Laurel's eyes turned blood red, and his nails turned into claws as he struggled to break free. Suddenly, there was a loud snap and Laurel stopped moving.

Aris and Kai both loosened their grips on the rope, letting Laurel's body slump to the ground. I breathed a sigh of relief as I stared at his lifeless body crumbling on the floor. Aris got to his feet and smiled when his eyes locked on Cira.

He crossed the distance towards her, scooping her into his arms and giving her a little twirl. She squeezed him tightly and laughed. They were both so happy, and I was happy for them, but something was wrong. They were so caught up in their moment they didn't notice, but I did.

I continued to stare at Laurel's body, just waiting but nothing happened. His body, oddly enough, remained completely intact. Was this what happened when you killed a half witch half vampire? When they died, did they not turn into ash like the rest of us?

Kai stepped away from his body and attempted to approach me, that's when I saw it. A slight twitch in Laurel's hand. Before I had a chance to warn Kai, Laurel reached out and grabbed Kai's ankle, tripping him before grabbing his leg and dragging him back towards him.

Laurel used his claws from his free hand to cut the rope around his ankles and his neck. The rope whipped past them both and slipped through the holding on the wall causing the chandelier above to drop.

"No!" I shouted racing toward them, but I had been bled too much and hadn't fed in days. I was weak and it felt like I was moving at half the speed of a normal human. I couldn't make it in time as the giant, glass monstrosity came crashing down, shards flying everywhere and crushing them both.

Chapter 25

I don't know why I chose to come back here. Looking at this empty compound that used to be filled with laughter and cheer, now it was filled with nothing but the haunting memories of my fallen comrades and their families. My family did this. My family who was being manipulated and terrorized by that psychotic ass witch, were responsible for all this hurt and destruction.

I walked past a photo that hung from the wall. A picture of Aris. He stood out in the training fields, dressed in his training armor. Black tunic, with bright gold buttons, lining his chest. Gold epaulettes on each shoulder, a brown leather belt around his waist which held his sword in place. He wore brown gloves on his hands as he stood proudly in front of the younger boys, he had been training, smiling brightly.

He looked magnificent and strong, and he looked like the perfect man to fall in love with.

What did fall in love with me get him though. Ripped away from his family, away from the life he used to have. It cost him a child and now he was imprisoned somewhere having who knows what done to him. I probably made his situation worse by escaping the witch.

I must find him and rescue my sister, but I wasn't even sure where to start my search.

As I stared at the picture, I racked my brain trying to figure out how I could find Aris. Over the years, I had learned that Aris was an amazing tracker, and it seemed as if his abilities had only been heightened after I had marked him to almost supernatural levels. Maybe if I could find him, he could help me find Kai.

Two marked humans and one immortal wouldn't be enough to take down one of the most powerful immortals, a hybrid and a witch, but at least if they didn't have any leverage over us, we would have a better chance of escape.

Since I had no clue where Aris was, or how to find him, my only option now was to see if I could somehow connect with him through the mark. The witch had already admitted to using a spell to disconnect our bond so I would believe her when she said he was dead, since then, I hadn't been able to connect with him.

Which one was a lie, was he dead or alive? I had to try again. Taking my eyes off the photo, I walked over to the large grey couch in the middle of the room. Sitting down, I pulled my legs up and crossed them in front of me. Closing my eyes, I took a deep breath and concentrated.

I opened my mind and tried to reach out to him. I let thoughts of him and some of my favorite memories of our time together flood every cell of my body. *Aris. Aris, where are you?*

Sweat formed on my brow with the amount of mental power I was exerting.

Aris? Please Aris, can you hear me? You must tell me where you are. I must know where you are.

I sat like that for I'm not sure how long, just trying with all my might for something, anything to at least prove to me he was alive, and they hadn't done something terrible to him just to punish me. I needed to hear him.

The wind outside blew through the trees, and I could hear the leaves rustling on the branches. I could smell their piney scent and hear the water from the small stream out back hitting the rocks as it rushed through. The few birds we had on the island chirped and I could feel the warmth of the sun on my face.

This compound was always so peaceful in the morning, and I use to be able to enjoy it with Aris, now I was sitting here all alone, hoping that we could share another morning like all the other ones.

Taking a deep breath, I let it out and tried again to reach my mind out to him and that's when I heard it. It was faint, but it was there. The faint thumping sound of a heartbeat. My eyes shot open and darted around the room. I expected to see someone else in the room with me, but there was no one.

I tried again, closed my eyes, and thought about Aris and the sound of the beating heart returned to my ears.

Aris.

I couldn't hear him, but it was almost like I could feel his heartbeat in my chest right next to mine. It was Aris, it had to be. He was alive and just like it has every single day we were together before, his heart was calling out to me. He wanted me to find him, even if something was preventing him from telling me.

I got to my feet, kept my eyes closed and just followed the sound of the heartbeat. I was putting a lot of faith into what I was hearing. This could be another trick by the witch just to set up a trap for me. Something in my heart told me that wasn't the case, this was Aris, and this sound was going to lead me right to him.

The sounds of nature grew louder once I'd exited the compound, but I tried to zone them out and focus completely on the thumping of the heartbeat.

Oddly enough, it seemed so loud suddenly, kind of like he was really close by. I walked a little further into the woods and only stopped when I ran face first into a tree. I took a step back and rubbed the sore spot that was now in the center of my forehead.

When I opened my eyes, I was staring at the trunk of a tree. I looked around, taking in my surroundings. This area looked incredibly familiar, this tree however, did not.

I looked up at the tree, it was huge and completely out of place. While there was mostly small shrubbery in this area, there were few trees. Just like most of the trees on this entire island, they were pine trees. This tree however had droopy branches, thick leaves, and the trunk was just slightly bigger than that of a pine tree.

That wasn't the only thing that was strange about this tree, it had a black trunk and bright red leaves. On this island, there were no such thing as seasons so tree leaves changing colors was not normal.

I closed my eyes again and tried listening for the thumping again. It took a second, but there it was again, just as strong as before. When I opened my eyes, I realized there was a reason I ran into the tree. It wasn't because the sound was coming from further into the forest and the tree was just blocking my path, it was because the sound was coming from inside the tree.

That couldn't be right, how could a heartbeat come from inside a tree. Taking a closer step to the tree, I ran my fingers along the rough texture of the bark.

Something was off about this tree. Walking around the tree, I noticed the thumping getting louder and faster. *Aris? Are you in there?*

I felt around the trunk until I got to one section of it that felt different, smoother. Pressing on that smooth section my hand slipped through and disappeared through the trunk. It was another one of the witch's illusions. The tree wasn't even real, it was just a way for the witch to be able to hide him right here in plain sight.

I pushed my hand further into the tree and then added my second one, feeling around for any obstacles. My hand touched something soft and warm. Exploring more, I felt skin and then fingers. *Aris.*

Wrapping my hand around the wrist attached to those fingers, I pulled. I saw his hand first, then his arm. I pulled and pulled until he collapsed into my arms. Losing my balance, I fell onto my back. Lucky for my superior strength, otherwise his large frame would crush me.

I sat up just enough to get a good look at his face. Brushing his hair from his face, I examined him, looking for any visible wounds. I couldn't see any, but he wasn't waking up. Giving him a couple light taps on the cheek didn't work, so I did the next best thing.

Tilting his head to the side, I let my fangs lengthen before pulling him close and sinking my fangs deep into the side of his neck. I felt his body jerk in my arms as I pulled on the vein and drew the succulent blood past my lips.

How I've missed this. His warm, sweet blood coating the back of my throat. His strong body in my arms, on top of me, I've missed it all. Pull after pull on the plump vein in his neck sent me further into a drugged up state. This is what his blood did to me, it was so good it made it so hard to stop.

The more I drank the more that special spot between my legs began to tingle. I couldn't help myself; I wanted him. I wasn't thinking about that stupid prophecy or how my own father tried to marry off both my sister and I just to benefit himself. I wasn't thinking about how much danger I had put the man that I love in, I wasn't even thinking about the danger my little sister was currently in. The only thing on my mind was him, us, in this moment and how much I wanted to feel his bare skin on mine, in me.

My mind was so out of it, I hadn't even noticed the moment he had slipped his arms around my waist. He pulled me close and matched the grinding motion of my hips with equal friction of his own. I moved my hips faster, my heart racing. I wanted this so bad, I needed it.

The pressure built, until it was almost unbearable, almost painful. I couldn't hold it anymore, I retracted my fangs from his neck, tightened my grip on him and let go. I couldn't tell who moaned louder, Aris or me.

My whole-body shook, and it took tremendous effort just to draw breath into my lungs. It seemed like a decade had gone by before I felt myself floating down from the cloud Aris had placed me on.

Aris rolled off me so he wouldn't have to put all his weight on me. I laid there unable to do the bare minimum like even opening my eyes. "That's some way to get someone to wake up." Aris joked.

I wanted to laugh, but as the high of what we just did began to wear off, the gravity of what we were facing began to resurface. Niyla, I needed to find a way to save her and the only way to even begin coming up with a plan would be to find Kai first. Nothing could be done unless we were sure there was no way they could have any kind of leverage on any of us. Once we were sure of that, we would destroy all three of them.

6 hours earlier

"Are you sure this is the best idea?" Aris and I stood in the tunnels below the castle. The same tunnels that helped us save my sister and her mate and this was the third time Aris had asked me that question.

I didn't like this anymore than he did, and I was already having tremendous doubts about it, but what other choice did we have, we needed a lead if we wanted to find Kai and save Niyla.

Some of the guards in the castle luckily were still loyal to me and my sister and didn't like the fact that a witch was calling the shots over the all-powerful and great Ezra Grey. I couldn't blame them, Ezra had always been horrible over the years, to find out he ran off every other race of creatures that use to inhabit this island. That was the kind of man he had always been, but the type to harm his own family, he was not, this was all that witch's doing. She had to go.

One of the guards, Caleb, who had helped us sneak into the tunnels before, had heard that there was a separate access tunnel connected to these caves that led to a small corridor that overlooked an underground lake. Considering how many times Niyla and I had explored these tunnels and had no idea about this secret passage, Aris and I figured it was a good place to start looking for clues to find Kai.

Now, we stood in the middle of this tunnel staring at a cave wall. A dead end. "There has to be something more than this." I took a step closer to the wall, but even with my enhanced eyesight it was extremely difficult to get a good look at it. It was probably another one of her tricks. This one seemed to be her favorite.

"What do we do now? I managed to track the trail this far, but it's like it completely disappeared right here and there's nothing but a dead end."

Running my fingers along the cold, rough wall, I came to another smooth patch. Just like the one on the tree where Aris was hidden and just like then, my hand was able to pass right through it.

I couldn't help the smile that spread on my face. She really needed some new tricks; it was just pathetic how predictable she was getting.

"Found it." I called back to Aris. I felt him walk up behind me so I stepped to the side so he could see my hand passing through the wall.

His eyes grew wide as he stared at it. "What is this? A trick from the witch."

I nodded my head. "Apparently it's her favorite one."

Reaching back, I grabbed Aris's hand and walked through the wall, making sure he came through with me. I wasn't sure how the witch's spells worked, and I didn't want to get separated traveling through some strange portal.

We emerged in another corridor really like the one we were just in. Dark, cold but unlike the other one, the walls of this one were wet. The temperature was a few degrees warmer and with the amount of humidity my skin felt sticky.

"I guess we're in the right place." Aris squeezed my hand tighter and walked ahead of me, leading me along. He ran his hand along the walls as we walked.

It didn't take us long to be dumped out into another large opening. Straight ahead of us was a huge opening that led to an overlook, to the left another tunnel and to the right a small opening. It looked like a cave.

"Which way?"

I looked back and forth between the two different directions, but I wasn't sure which way was the right way, and I didn't want to waste unnecessary time checking both.

"You check the left, I'll go right."

Aris hesitated but agreed. He lifted our combined hands to his lips and gave it a little peck before releasing it and heading toward the tunnel. I watched him disappear into the shadows before turning and heading for the cave. I made sure to keep my hands on the sides of the walls, just to make sure I wasn't going to fall into another one of the witch's traps. This part of the cave was much colder then part we entered, how was that possible?

"Kai?" I called out. It was a risk to try calling out to him, who knows what lurked in these tunnels. For all I knew, the witch could be lying in wait, and I could be letting her know where I was right now. I couldn't think about that now though, we were on a time limit. If the witch was able to remove the mark,

I'm sure Ezra would want to go ahead with the wedding right away. If Niyla marked Laurel, there would be no going back.

"Kai?" I called out again but this time, I was meant with a slight, haggard cough. So, I tried again. "Kai? Are you in here?" Another cough.

I squinted my eyes trying to force them to adjust as much as they could to the terrible lighting. I saw a dark figure crouching in a corner. It was so still, for a second I was concerned it was part of the cave wall, and I was just imagining things.

"Kai? Is that you?"

There was a groan followed by another cough. I inhaled deeply. I hadn't been around Kai enough to be able to recognize his scent, but I could recognize that it was a human. I decided to throw caution aside. Rushing toward the figure, I crouched down trying to get a good look at them.

Rolling him over so he was flat on his back, there was barely enough lighting to catch a glimpse of his face. Kai. I breathed a sigh of relief. I'd found him and with any luck, I'd done it in enough time to stop the wedding and save my sister.

"Cira!" Aris shouted my name. I turned around just in time to see him running towards me. He stopped just a few steps away and held up something. A book?

"What is that?" I asked. It shimmered gold and red in the dim lighting like it was made from solid gold and rubies.

"You need to see this, it's everything about the witch's history. Her origin, what gives her, her powers and best of all, her weaknesses."

I shot up to my feet. "Her weaknesses?"

Aris nodded then flipped the book open, pointing to a spot on the page that he stopped on. "This book tells us how to kill her. All we need is a little holy water and that psycho bitch is dead."

Chapter 26

Cira grabbed me, knocking us both to the ground as shards of glass from the broken chandelier flew in every direction. A large cloud of dust engulfed us, making it difficult to see anything. Cira rolled off me and quickly got to her feet.

"Aris?" She called out trying to wade her way through the thick cloud. A thick cloud that made seeing Kai impossible. I scrambled to my feet and went after her, holding out my arms as I went.

The smoke began to clear, and I managed to find Cira. The sight before us had us frozen stiff. Aris lay unmoving on the floor with the chandelier sitting right on his chest. A small pile of ash laid at his side and Kai at his other, his arm trapped under part of the chandelier. Laurel was nowhere to be found; I could only assume that pile of ash was all that was left of him.

In a flash both Cira and I were at their sides. I grabbed one end of the chandelier and indicated for Cira to grab the other end and together we were able to lift it off them. I kneeled next Kai, sliding him over and placing his head on my lap, lightly tapping his face.

"Kai! Kai! Please Kai wake up." There was a huge gash on the side of his head right near his temple and blood was practically gushing from it. My cheeks were wet, and my vision was blurry from the tears that didn't seem to want to stop.

"Aris please!" Cira screamed. She sat a few feet away from me, next to Aris. Kai should be the one in that position. He was standing right underneath the chandelier; Aris must've pushed him out of the way causing him to take the brunt of the impact. Aris had sacrificed himself for us. Her hands hovered over his body like she was afraid to touch him because she wasn't sure if she would make his injuries worse.

From my distance I could see Aris' eyes open slowly. His lips moved but no words came out. Cira dropped her head, so her ear was close to Aris' mouth. "Aris, just a little louder baby." I was just barely able to make out what he said.

"Can't. Breathe."

Cira lifted her head, staring wide eyed at him, then turned her head to look at me. Cursing under my breath, I gently placed Kai's head back on the floor, scooting closer to Cira and Aris.

My eyes ran over his body, it didn't take a genius to figure out what was wrong.

There were dark purple bruises on his neck that disappeared beyond his shirt and probably covered his chest. I swallowed hard. "Cira, I think it crushed his lungs."

Her lip quivered as she turned back to face him. She hesitated before reaching out to grab him, but I grabbed her arm to stop her.

"What are you doing?" I asked.

"We need to get him help." I could hear the desperation evident in her voice, which meant she wasn't thinking clearly.

"If you move him, you risk making it worse. Even with your speed, there's no way you can get him to a hospital in enough time. We don't even have any doctors that can treat a human on the island." There was no way to sugar coat this situation, it didn't look good and because Cira was mated to Aris and could only drink his blood, if he died, she died.

"So, what am I supposed to do? Let him die?" My mind raced a mile a minute as I tried to come up with a reasonable solution. Some way so I wouldn't have to lose my sister, and she wouldn't lose her mate. There was only one answer that kept coming to mind. One I was nervous to suggest since I wasn't sure if it was something they had ever discussed with each other.

I tried swallowing the lump that was beginning to form in my throat before I spoke. "The mark isn't going to heal him fast enough, his injuries are too bad. There is one thing you could do but you need to make sure it is something that he would want."

I could see Cira's body visibly stiffen as she took in my words. She glanced at Aris, who was still struggling to breathe. A steady stream of blood began dribbling from the corner of his mouth. He was dying right before our eyes. She needed to decide right now before it was too late.

"But..." She started but let her words trail off.

"There is no other choice Cira, unless you want to sit here and watch your mate suffer and die knowing there was something you could've done to prevent it." I know I was being harsh and even pushy, but I couldn't risk losing her again, I had just gotten her back. So, if that meant pushing her into changing Aris' life forever then that's what I was going to do. I didn't care if I was being selfish.

Cira didn't reply, she just nodded and gently lifted Aris' head off the floor to place it on her lap. She gave me one last quick glance before focusing all her attention on the man in her arms struggling to breathe.

Tilting Aris' head back slightly she leaned in and whispered to him, "I'm sorry." Just as a single tear rolled down her cheek. I felt for my sister, but it had to be done. Another tear slipped from her eyes just as her fangs eased out of her gums and she latched on to Aris' neck.

I could feel Aris jerk slightly when my fangs pierced his neck. Tear after tear slid down my cheek as almost every drop of his blood filled my mouth. I didn't want to be doing this, taking his life away from him but I didn't have a choice. I'm doing this for my own selfish reasons, so I wouldn't have to walk this Earth without him, even if it was only for a short time. I wanted us to be able to live our lives together, to have the children that we never got to have, to experience the happiness that the fear of being caught had kept from us.

We had never talked about Aris being turned before; we've never had a need to. For all I knew this could be the worst thing to happen to him. After being used as a blood slave for all those years in the castle before I marked him, he could hate the idea of having to live off blood for the rest of his existence.

Taking almost all his blood, I pulled away only to sink my fangs into my bare wrist. Blood oozed from the punctured wounds, and I placed them to Aris' mouth urging him to drink. Aris resisted a little but finally gave in. Once I was satisfied that he'd consumed enough of my blood, it was time for the final step of the change. The step I really didn't know if I could handle doing.

Placing my hands on either side of Aris' face, I looked at his eyes, they were barely open now, like it took everything in him to keep them open. I gave him my best reassuring smile and gave him a slight nod to let him know that everything would be okay, even if I wasn't fully sure myself.

Aris closed his eyes, squeezing them tight. I took a deep breath before giving his head one hard twist causing his neck to snap, killing him instantly.

My hands shook violently. The moment I had done it, it felt like my heart had been ripped out of my chest. I couldn't control my tears or the nonstop sobs. I told myself repeatedly that he would be fine, that he was just taking a little nap, but nothing seemed to work. I had killed my love, and it tore my heart to shreds.

I knew he would wake up in a couple of hours or days and be perfectly fine, but seeing him not moving, not breathing, and knowing I was the cause of it shattered me.

I felt the light touch of a hand on my shoulder. Turning around, I was immediately embraced in a tight hug. Niyla whispered soothing words in my ear and stroked my hair, reminding me that he was only sleeping and when he woke up, we would have an eternity together.

I wasn't sure how long we had been sitting in our little embrace. Eventually Cira pulled away and said she was fine now. That gave me the opportunity to go back to attending to Kai.

He had awoken sometime during our embrace but knew better than to get up right away. The bump on his head had gotten even bigger and the cut was still bleeding badly. He cradled his arm to his chest and from the way his shoulder looked, the entire arm was likely dislocated.

"I need to take you to see one of the physicians we have they're not really equipped to deal with humans, but they might be able to help at least a little."

Kai shooed my hands away so I would stop trying to help him up. He looked up at me. "You don't need to worry about me, oddly I'm not in as much pain as I thought I would be." Maybe because he was still marked and had been growing in strength, his body had developed the ability to heal a lot faster than any other human.

"What about you?" He asked. "He cut you pretty deep." Pulling my hair over my shoulder, I showed Kai my neck where there was just the tiniest cut left, no bigger than the average paper cut.

"See, I'm fine." He sighed a little and gave me a small smile, but it quickly disappeared, and he suddenly refused to look at me.

"So, what happens now?" My face scrunched up into one of confusion.

"What do you mean?" I asked.

"You told me that none of this was real, your feelings for me, the reason you marked me, all of it was a lie."

I dropped my head in shame. Even if I had told him all of that to protect him, I still regret that I had to say it. I needed him to know the truth about how I felt and what better time than after the two of us almost died.

"Everything I told you, was a lie. The witch threatened us, threatened you. I had to make you believe my feelings for you weren't real, but I guess I failed."

Kai looked up at me, right into my eyes. "And how do you know you've failed." The defiant look in his eyes might've done its job if I didn't already know the truth.

I smiled at him before reaching out and grabbing his chin, turning his head sideways. There, clear as it's ever been, was the mark. No sign that it had disappeared even a little, no fading, nothing. My heart sped up when I stared at it. He loved me, even if he was too angry with me to admit it right now.

"If you truly believed what I said and your feelings for me had changed, the witch's spell would've worked and the marked would've disappeared." I released his chin and let him turn his head back to face me.

"If you're still marked by me, my feelings for you should be evident, but in case they aren't I'm going to spell it out for you." I took a deep breath and grabbed his hand. He stared at our interlaced fingers before meeting my eyes again. "Stowing away on your ship and finding myself in your... capable hands," Kai laughed and squeezed my hand. "It wasn't on purpose, but maybe it wasn't by accident either. There was a reason I meant you when I needed you most and I like to think of it as fate."

Pulling my hand from his I gently slipped them both around his neck, pulling him closer. "In the short time that we've known each other you've managed to catch my heart in your little sailor's net, and I haven't been able to escape since. Face it Captain Kaiel, you're stuck with me."

His smile grew wider, and he pulled me close, so our lips were just barely touching, "I love you too." He whispered.

Just before his lips touched mine, we were interrupted. "You insolent girls." The disgust I heard in that voice could've only come from one person. Looking up I see Ezra standing in the doorway with his arms folded.

Narrowing my eyes at him, I got to my feet, stepping in front of Kai. "This is over Ezra; Laurel is dead and so is the witch. Your plan has failed, and you have no reason to keep my sister and I here."

He chuckled. "Of course, you would believe that, but this was simply just a hiccup in my plans. Nothing has been lost to me yet."

He made a move to take a step towards us, and I braced myself for a fight, but before he could take a step, he was slammed into the wall.

"Leave!" My mother shouted at us as she pressed Ezra's body further into the wall.

I stared at her in confusion before turning back to look at Cira who shared the same confused look.

"Lilianna, what do you think you're doing?" Ezra ground his teeth together as he tried to fight against our mother, but surprisingly enough she seemed to be overpowering him.

"You, my love, have lied and manipulated me for centuries. It was your decision alone to cast out my daughter and your decision to imprison the other. It was even solely your choice to not perform the marking ritual and now I find out it is because you had a desire to mark that witch."

My eyes grew wide at this revelation. I had always assumed my parents had marked each other when they got married. It's usually part of the ceremony.

"If not for the risk of her powers being effected, you would've marked her years ago is that not right darling." The cracks in the concrete walls deepened as my mother pressed harder. "We were supposed to rule together, but now I see that is not an option to you. I will not allow you to harm them anymore for your own selfish gain." She turned to face us. "I said leave! Now! Do not come back."

Epilogue

"Of course, I would find you here." Kai said as he walked up behind me, wrapping his arms around me and pulling me close.

The deep blue water surrounding us seemed to stretch on forever with no end in sight. The wind that blew through my hair smelled clean and fresh and I loved to breathe it in deep so I could fill my lungs with as much of it as possible.

It had been over a week since we escaped the castle. Just like when I left home before, we stowed away on a ship at the docks. We made it to the next closest island where we were lucky enough to run into an old friend of Kai's. He gave us aid back to Kai's home where Cira and Aris decided to stay for the time being. I of course followed my mate back aboard his ship to continue with his duties.

Life seemed normal yet not at the same time. I liked to come out to the front of the ship and just watch the water so I could collect my thoughts. There was so much to think about after all. I was worried my father would make another attempt to come after us. I was worried what he would do to my mother for defying him. Most of all I couldn't stop thinking about what Cira had told me.

Ezra had banished hundreds of other species from their homes just for his own power trip. There were others forced from their homes the same way I was.

I may not be able to bring back the lives that were lost during that time, but I wondered if there was some way, I could help them get their homes back.

"I can tell when your mind is racing a mile a minute even without reading it." Kai leaned in and gently kissed the side of my neck, sending a shiver down my spine. "Are you thinking of the different excuses we could use so we can go back to bed for the rest of the day."

His breath against my skin and the seductive way he spoke caused my skin to break out into goosebumps and my knees to buckle a little.

I turned in his arms so I could wrap my arms around his neck. I leaned in and placed a gently kiss on his lips.

"As tempting as that is, no that's not what has my mind preoccupied." I stared at a spot on his chest and gently bit my lip.

"I know you very much enjoy your time onboard your ship but how would feel about returning my home back to its former glory." Kai pulled away slightly. "We wouldn't be away forever; I just want to give those who were forced out, their homes back."

Kai reached up and shelved my chin on his hand, forcing me to look at him. "I figured this was something you would bring up eventually, that's just the type of person you are. Of course, I would follow you anywhere because that's who I am." The smile that spread across my face was almost enough to hurt my face. I loved this man, and I would continue to for all eternity. It was clear there was nothing we couldn't do if we were together.